Clarence Cochran,
A Human Boy

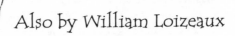

Also by William Loizeaux

FOR YOUNG READERS

Wings

ADULT NONFICTION

Anna: A Daughter's Life

The Shooting of Rabbit Wells

Clarence Cochran,
A Human Boy

William Loizeaux

Pictures by
Anne Wilsdorf

Melanie Kroupa Books

Farrar Straus Giroux
New York

Text copyright © 2009 by William Loizeaux
Illustrations copyright © 2009 by Anne Wilsdorf
All rights reserved
Printed in the United States of America
Distributed in Canada by Douglas & McIntyre Ltd.
Designed by Jonathan Bartlett
First edition, 2009
10   9   8   7   6   5   4   3   2   1

www.fsgkidsbooks.com

Library of Congress Cataloging-in-Publication Data
Loizeaux, William.
    Clarence Cochran, a human boy / William Loizeaux ; pictures by Anne
Wilsdorf.— 1st ed.
        p.   cm.
    Summary: With the threat of extermination looming, a cockroach who
has been transformed into a tiny human learns to communicate with his
human hosts, leading to an agreement both sides can live with, and a
friendship between Clarence and ten-year-old Mimi, a human
environmentalist.
    ISBN-13: 978-0-374-31323-4
    ISBN-10: 0-374-31323-7
    [1. Cockroaches—Fiction.   2. Toleration—Fiction.   3. Change—
Fiction.   4. Environmental protection—Fiction.]   I. Wilsdorf, Anne, ill.
II. Title.

PZ7.L8295 Cla 2009
[Fic]—dc22

                                                              2007035358

For Beth and Emma

Clarence Cochran,
A Human Boy

1 / The Change

When young Clarence Cochran woke from disturbing dreams one evening, something seemed to have changed. True, he was lying in his familiar crevice in the wall behind the top shelf, high above the Gilmartins' stove and refrigerator. But that evening, his head felt different, oddly large, yet light. He shook it, but nothing arched or swayed gracefully in front of him. *That's strange,* he thought, *I can't see my antennae.* Then he looked down at the rest of his body. What he saw made him sit bolt upright. *What has become of me?*

Gone were the dark brown ridges on his belly. Gone were the tiny airholes along his sides through

which he normally breathed. Gone were the two stiff hairs on the rear of his abdomen that warned him of trouble creeping up from behind— usually Floyd, one of his older brothers, who liked to tease and push him around.

He twisted his head to look behind him. Gone, as well, were his beautiful wings. But worst of all, where were his six trusty and many-jointed barbed legs that helped him scurry over the kitchen floor, up the walls, and upside down across the ceiling?

Clarence closed his eyes and wished he could go back to sleep. He'd been just fine that morning when he'd crawled deep down into his crevice and his mother had listened to his prayers and put him to bed. So maybe all this was just a dream. Maybe when he really and truly woke up, he'd be his old cockroach self again.

"Clar-ence!" his mother called from the shelf just below, where his family usually gathered before going down to the counters to eat and where the Gilmartins, their human hosts, still had three yellowing cook-books and a wooden box full of recipes no one had used in years. Kathryn Gilmartin, the wife, mother, and family breadwinner, didn't have much time for cooking anymore. And Larry Gilmartin, her hus-band, who was in charge of the kitchen and walked their daughter Mimi to and from school, had about as much interest in cooking as he did in cleaning up afterward. His specialties were hot dogs, instant mashed potatoes, delivered pizza, and Chinese take-out.

"Clar-ence? I don't hear you stirring up there!" Clarence's mother called again in her cheery, musical voice. The evenings always made her happy and ea-ger for the nightly search for food with her family. "Rise and shine!" she went on. "Up an' at 'em! Your father is waiting, hungry as a bear. And Floyd and Stephen are already down here, too. You don't want them hogging all the sweet-and-sour pork, do you?"

Clarence knew his brothers were up. He couldn't hear them yawning and grumbling in their sleeping places nearby on the top shelf. If he didn't get going, Floyd and Stephen *would* eat all the sweet-and-sour sauce and whatever remained of the fortune cookies! In a voice that came out more squeaky than normal, he yelled, "Coming!" Then, screwing up his courage, he opened his eyes in the dim light and looked again at his sorry self.

Inexplicably, a pair of plaid boxer shorts, the kind that humans wear, encircled his waist and hips. The rest of him was covered in skin the color of uncooked chicken, with bits of blond fuzz here and there. His body wasn't any longer, but it looked like it had stretched. And what had happened to his shell, with its rich brown color and hard finish? How could it be gone? How would he hold himself together? His legs—he could only count four, not six, of them now!—had become long, smooth tubes. And at the ends of each, five smaller tubes had sprouted, each ridiculously short and stubby.

With some relief, Clarence *did* notice one tiny,

lonely hole in the middle of his abdomen, just above the elastic waistband of his shorts. Yet he didn't seem to be breathing through it, and it wasn't giving off that pleasant, stinky, and reassuring odor that usually made him feel at peace with the world and at one with his family.

Wondering about the rest of himself that he couldn't see, he clumsily stretched one of his strange front legs toward his head and then touched it. His head *was* bigger! He felt short thick hair that swirled and stuck up in the back, then a fleshy, shell-shaped thing that led into a waxy tunnel. On the front, he felt eyes, like grapes, sunk into deep sockets. Between them was a bump with two small holes, each with yucky, gooey gunk inside. He felt an oval mouth in which the parts worked oddly up and down and where a damp, flat, noodley thing flopped this way and that. "Hold on, I'll be right there!" he shouted, his voice still sounding squeaky.

"What, has the kid got a cold or something?" That was Clarence's father, who wasn't exactly at his best in the evenings before he got some food into him. He, too, was on the shelf below.

Then Clarence heard his mother reply, "Well, maybe he *does* have a cold or a fever. Poor child. I'll go up and see. It isn't like him to be so late."

"Tell him to move his precious little butt!" That was his annoying brother Floyd speaking.

"You mind your own business," his mother said to Floyd. "I'll handle this."

Clarence heard the soft patter of her steps as she climbed toward his crevice along the cupboard wall. Soon she was on the top shelf.

"No! Wait! Don't come in here!" he cried. He didn't want his mother, or anyone for that matter, to see him like this. If he could just hold her off a little longer, he might find a way to get back to his normal self.

"You all right?" she asked him gently, still out of sight.

"Yes! I'll be there in a minute!"

He heard his mother pause, then turn around.

"Well, get a move on!" his father called up to him.

"Let's go!" cried Stephen, who ordinarily paid more attention to preening his long wings and antennae than he ever did to Clarence. "I have an appointment," he announced, which meant that later he'd be meeting Martha McMoffit again, strolling with her, wing-to-wing, along the shadowy path beneath the radiator.

"Hurry along, Clarence," his mother called, more sharply than before.

Now Clarence tried to get on his legs and crawl out of the crevice. Usually this was easy. With his six strong, spiky legs and sticky claws, he'd scoot right up the steep, almost vertical wall of wood and crumbling plaster.

On this evening, though, everything was more complicated. He had no middle legs, and his smooth hind legs were absolutely worthless for climbing. Just looking at them made him feel faint. Still, with much awkward shoving and slithering, he moved his body from its lying-down position at the bottom of the crevice so that his stomach leaned against the sloped wall and the ends of his front legs could grab onto a narrow ridge. With all his might, he tried to pull himself up so he could see over the rim. But soon his front legs shook and weakened, until he slid sadly down the wall, splinters sticking into his stomach.

He tried to climb up again and again, but it didn't work. Exhausted, he slid down and collapsed on his back. Hopelessly, he looked up at the dark walls, as if from the bottom of an open grave. *How will I ever get out of here?*

2 / What *Is* It?

That's when his mother's heart-shaped face, the face Clarence had known since he'd hatched as a wingless, naked nymph, appeared over the rim of the crevice. She must have heard his struggling. "Clarence?" She was peering down at him. "Is that you?"

He wasn't sure. "Yes, Mom, it's me—I guess," he said in a frail tone.

Her eyes went wide, and her head and antennae began to quiver. She let out a gasp: "Oh, my goodness!"

"What's going on up there?" came his father's irritated voice.

In seconds, Clarence heard the sound of feet scampering up the cupboard wall, onto the top shelf, past an old ball of string, through a grove of dusty wineglasses, over a tar-nished candlesnuffer, and around the strange, ceramic teapot, shaped like a tropical bird.

Soon Clarence saw his father, Stephen, and Floyd, along with his mother, peering down from the rim of the crevice.

"Who's *that*?" his father asked.

"What *is* it?" his brothers said together.

"I think something's happened to Clarence," his mother replied. She was sniffling and weeping tears the size of dewdrops. "He doesn't look right."

"I'll say!" said Floyd.

"How do you even know it's him?" his father asked.

"I heard him speak," she said. "It was *his* voice. I

heard him say 'Mom.' And those eyes! Look at them. They couldn't be anyone else's!"

"Are you sure?" Clarence's father said in disbelief.

Floyd, always the courageous one, took a few steps down the wall of the crevice to see Clarence more clearly. Like their father, he was stocky and short-winged, almost like a beetle. You wouldn't think he'd be a natural on vertical surfaces, but the barbs on his legs were supersharp. He could cling to almost anything. "Check out its color," Floyd called back to the others. "Ewww!"

Grimacing, Stephen covered his eyes with one claw. "How can you even stand to look at it?"

As you might imagine, this was terribly upsetting to Clarence. He'd always known he was a little different from his brothers and most other roaches. He was quiet and shy. Some called him "dreamy." Like everyone in his family, he loved to eat, yet he wouldn't race each evening to be the first to the food. He wouldn't scuffle with the others and scramble over them. He liked sitting on the windowsill, watching the moon drift over the courtyard. He liked gazing at the labels on cans and bottles on the counters, and imagining shapes—a butterfly, a curly caterpillar—in the fascinating marks he saw on them. He'd never told anyone about this, but sometimes, as he studied those marks, he thought they were trying to speak to him. He'd imagine each mark making a sound, and together they'd make bigger sounds. But he couldn't understand what they were saying.

So he was, as his mother always said, "an unusual little fellow." Though never as unusual as *this*.

Lying on his back in the crevice, he tried to cry out, *Guys! It's me, Clarence!* Instead, fear and alarm clogged his throat. All he could do was grunt.

"Listen, he's trying to speak!" his mother said, drying her eyes. "We need to help him!"

"No, it's getting ready to do something nasty,"

Floyd said. "It's probably some weird wasp or snake, and you know what they like to do to us."

"Edith," Clarence's father put in, "something funny's going on here. I don't like the looks of this . . ." He nodded toward Clarence. "Or *that*."

"What are you talking about?" his mother snapped. "*That* is our *son* down there!"

"Let's get out of here!" Stephen groaned. "Everyone else is out on the counters."

"All right," Clarence's mother said, glaring at her two oldest sons, "if that's your idea of brotherly love, then go. Just go! All of you. But I'm staying here to help him!"

"Be reasonable," Clarence's father said, patting the top of her head. "Look at the poor creature. No wings. No antennae. No middle legs. That can't be Clarence. It can't even be a cockroach. Clarence must be down below already with the others, chowing down the egg rolls. Maybe he snuck off early with his pal Willie."

While his mother shook her head at this—her youngest son was hardly the sneaky type—Clarence's father continued, "Come on, let's get some breakfast." He glanced at Clarence. "Maybe *it*, or whatever *that* is, will be gone when we get back."

"You heard me," Clarence's mother said firmly. "I'm staying. Go ahead and suit yourselves. Leave if you must."

And so they did—or at least Clarence's brothers did.

More slowly, Clarence's father turned and started to move away.

If only he could know it's me! Clarence thought, and with great effort, managed to say, "Dad?" It was barely a whisper.

"Did you hear that?" his mother asked.

For a moment, his father stood silently, peering at Clarence with astonished eyes. Then, turning to Clarence's mother, he said, "I'd better get the doctor."

3 / Deliverance

When the sound of his father's steps had faded, Clarence's mother crept down the wall of the crevice in that hushed and watchful way that you approach the very ill. She was not what you would call a beautiful mother, but she had a graceful way of carrying her slender body. She studied Clarence, who stared back at her with his big, confused, and pleading eyes that seemed to be saying, *Mom, what's happened to me?*

And her own eyes seemed to be answering, *Honey, I wish I knew.* Halfway down the wall, she reached out her antennae and touched his shoulder, a touch he would have recognized anywhere. It reminded him of when he was sick with a fever, and she would cup her claw over his head, and that alone would make him feel better. Now she slowly moved her antennae over his ears, eyes, nose, mouth, and down his neck, careful of the splinters on his chest and stomach. She paid special attention to that hole in his middle.

"That's the strangest thing of all," she mused. "That and those silly shorts."

He knew he must be as disgusting to her as he was to himself. Still, she didn't cringe or back away. Instead, she came down to the bottom of the crevice.

"How do you feel?" she asked softly.

"Different," he said, his voice still weak.

She reached out her claw and opened it against his forehead. After a moment, she said, "You're warm, but you don't have a fever. Do you want to rest?"

"Yes, but not here," he said. Usually the crevice was his favorite place in the whole world. He fit so snugly into it, and Floyd seldom bothered him here. Now, however, it seemed cramped, stuffy, and dingy. He had a yearning for wider spaces. "I'd like some fresh air," he said.

This was an unusual request. It made his mother cock her head. "You sure?"

He nodded.

"Okay," she said. "But first, don't you want to get out of those shorts? They can't be very comfortable around your legs like that."

Now Clarence felt another strange thing. He felt very attached to his shorts, and the idea of taking them off in anyone's presence, including his mother's, filled him with fear and shame. "I think I'll keep them on," he said.

"Okay," she said again. Then she added, "What about those splinters? You don't want to keep those, do you?"

"No," he said, relieved that they'd found an area of agreement.

"Good. Let's see if we can take care of them." She bent over him and, operating her claws like tweezers, drew the splinters bit by bit from his skin. This hurt, but bravely he clenched the ends of his front legs and tried not to cry out or whimper.

"There," she said a while later. "Phew! All done. Feel better?"

"A little."

She took a step back, as if to consider the situation, weigh their options, and make a decision. "All right," she said, "now here's what we're going to do." She bent all six of her legs accordian-style, collapsing them, and lowered herself as flat as a rug. "Roll over onto my back," she said. "We used to do this when you were a nymph. Remember?"

Twisting and pushing, Clarence rocked his body side to side, and finally managed to roll onto her back, stomach down. With a pang, he breathed in her rich scent, like blue cheese, and felt her thin, lacy wings.

"Grab onto my shoulders with your front legs, or

whatever they are," she said. "Wrap your hind ones around my shell."

He did this, more or less centering himself on her back. He was almost as big as she was.

Then, knee by knee and leg by leg, his mother raised herself up. With a flick of her head, she tossed her antennae up over the rim, like a couple of grappling hooks.

"Hang on," she said, "tight as a tick." And then, leaning into the slope, pulling hard on her antennae, she carried her son up and out of the crevice.

4 / A Boy

Near the front edge of the top shelf, Clarence's mother gently slid him into a measuring spoon that had once been misplaced by the Gilmartins. To be exact, it was a teaspoon, and in it Clarence sat with his back perfectly cradled and his legs, from the knees down, hanging over the edge.

"Comfortable?" she asked as she went to get a bit of damp cloth to cool his forehead. He breathed the air that wafted through the screened window above the sink, gazed out on the moonlit kitchen, and nodded yes.

The Gilmartins lived in apartment #518 on the west side of a square seven-story building. Their windows overlooked a grassy, enclosed courtyard which, while he could often hear the sounds of traffic, made Clarence feel that the city was far away. In a building where safe housing was difficult to find, the Gilmartins' kitchen had always been a good place for a cockroach family. Neighbors were numerous and friendly. A garbage can overflowed in the cabinet beneath the sink. A humming refrigerator motor could keep you warm all winter. The faucet dripped steadily, providing drinking water. And on the kitchen table stood a sticky sugar bowl and a lamp with a beaded pull-string, where Clarence liked to swing back and forth with Willie, his best friend.

Most important, though, the Gilmartins were generous and reliable hosts, who, for all these years, had been unaware that they were hosts at all. When Larry did cook, he was extremely messy. Dinner spills pooled on the stove top and stayed there until the next morning. When the dishwasher was full, entire plates of half-eaten hot dogs or fried wontons oozing in grease, along with bowls of melted ice cream—all of it in luscious, drooling mounds—would grace the countertops!

From his measuring spoon, Clarence looked out on this scene of peace and plenty, which included his brothers, neighbors, aunts, uncles, cousins, and Willie, too. Like Clarence, Willie was rather small and shy. He had no other close friends, so the two of them would always stick together. Seeing Willie down there reminded Clarence that he was missing all the excitement of the evening meal: the two of them like explorers, climbing into open cartons of Chinese food, searching for their own shred of pork or a secret puddle of curdled sauce in the curve of a noodle. But considering his unusual appearance, Clarence also felt relieved that he *wasn't* down there, having to explain himself. What would Willie think of him now?

He was wondering about this and feeling glum, when his father returned, climbing onto the far end of the shelf and carrying a small bag made from a scrap of black felt. From behind his father came the sounds of someone climbing very slowly up the wall. Listening closely, Clarence could distinguish the steps of five feet, along with the sharp tap of something else.

Now and then, the sounds would pause, and soon Clarence heard heavy breathing and a deep voice complaining, "Ralph, you didn't tell me your place was up so high. These walls are killing me!"

"You want a lift?" Clarence's father called back over the edge of the shelf.

"This is why I don't make house calls anymore!" came the voice. "This better be awfully important, not just a common cold or something!"

Of course, it was Dr. Blatt who finally hauled his whole self over the edge, the last thing being his shiny metal cane, which in fact was a tiny fishhook gripped upside down with his hind leg, the one that didn't have arthritis. For all the world, he looked like *he* could use a doctor. He was huffing and puffing. He was almost as wide as he was long. Though his favorite advice was "moderation," he'd seldom practiced it himself.

"Can I get you a bite to eat?" Clarence's mother, who appeared behind him, asked the doctor. For emergencies, she always kept some tasty bits of stale saltines and moldy Swiss cheese in the old box of wooden toothpicks behind the teapot.

"No, thanks," he said, still catching his breath, "I'm

on a diet." To Clarence's father, he said, "I'll take my bag now." Then, spying Clarence, he said, "So this is the patient, huh?"

While Clarence's father moved to the far end of the shelf—he was always uncomfortable around sickness—Dr. Blatt looked at Clarence with his keen, knowing, and now very interested eyes. From the bag, he pulled out a homemade surgical mask and tied it around his head.

Dr. Blatt, as he'd be happy to tell you, was an authority on many diseases. Like other professionals in the cockroach community, he'd learned his craft by imitating humans, in his case a doctor with an office in apartment #103, where he'd lived before moving to the Gilmartins'. And like many human doctors, Dr. Blatt had certain things he was good at, though his bedside manner wasn't one of them.

"I've seen some weird cases in my day," he said, still peering at Clarence with mounting excitement, "but this takes the cake!" He took a few steps forward and said aloud, "Patient presents with pallid exoskeleton, possibly molting; emaciated thorax; amputated cerci, tarsi, and antennae; pronotum and spiracles nonexistent."

Clarence
could often figure
out the meaning of words
he'd never heard, but these
were *very* mysterious. *What is he
talking about?*

"Remarkable!" the doctor said.

All this made Clarence shrivel down into the spoon.

Looming over him, the doctor got out his stetho-
scope, fashioned from thin copper wire. Murmuring
"Hmmmm . . . curious, hmmmm . . . interesting," he

held the cold circular end of the instrument on various parts of Clarence's chest and asked him to take deep breaths. "Say ahhhhh," he told Clarence, and then looked into his mouth. He searched Clarence's scalp for signs of antennae. He poked and pushed at Clarence's stomach. He even lifted the elastic waistband and glanced under Clarence's boxer shorts. Never had Clarence been so humiliated!

So it was with secret delight that Clarence watched the bottom half of his left leg do something all on its own. When the doctor tapped Clarence's knee, the leg shot up and kicked the cane right out from under the doctor's rear end. This caused the esteemed Dr. Blatt to tumble over onto his back, his legs wiggling in the air.

This, in turn, caused Clarence's mother to giggle in spite of herself.

Which, in turn, caused Dr. Blatt, when he'd finally rolled himself back onto his feet, to say to her, "There's nothing funny here at all! You, especially, have nothing to laugh at!" He paused, as if to enjoy the full return of his balance and authority. "In fact, I'm afraid I have some sobering news." He glared at her. "Your son will have to be quarantined. And so will you, in case you're already infected by whatever has caused his condition. Both of you are probably contagious. The entire community is at risk. As for you, Ralph, you've wisely kept your distance, so the quarantine need not apply to you."

"Quarantine?" Clarence's mother asked.

The doctor backed well away from the two of them and pulled down his surgical mask. "Yes! For forty days, you and your son must be isolated. You'll have to live here alone. And for everyone else, the top shelf will be off-limits." Dragging one of his gimpy legs, the doctor drew a long line in the dust, parallel to and about an inch away from the edge of the shelf. "You can't leave here," he went on. "You can't go over this line. Only doctors and emergency workers are allowed on *this* side, as well as someone to bring food and water. Of course, I will personally oversee the case and from time to time examine the patient. But otherwise, the two of you can have no contact with the rest of us."

"But why?" Clarence's father asked, bewildered.

"What's wrong with our son?" his mother said, her voice shaking.

The doctor stroked his chin thoughtfully. "I don't

quite know how to put this to you. I've never made this diagnosis before. It's highly unusual. Very intriguing . . ."

"Why don't you just put it to us directly and plainly?" Clarence's mother said with a hint of annoyance in her voice.

"All right." The doctor patted his brow with a handkerchief. "Plainly stated, your son is very sick, in grave condition, stricken by a terrible disease. What you have here is . . ." He paused. "Are you sure you want to know? It's horrible news."

"Yes," Clarence's mother said. "He's our son."

The doctor cleared his throat, then started again. "What you have here is . . . Well, it's not a cockroach . . . It's not the Clarence you've loved and nurtured . . . What you have here is . . ." Then finally he said it: "What you have is a little human . . . a boy."

5 / The Light

In a tight-knit community like the one in the Gilmartins' kitchen, big family news was hard to keep private, and this news was certainly no exception. Rumors had already started and spread like wildfire. Something mysterious had happened at the Cochrans'. Possibly some gruesome disease or injury. Possibly a miracle! Possibly a catastrophe! Why had Ralph, Clarence's father, begged Dr. Blatt to go up there? Why hadn't Edith, Clarence's mother, and Clarence come down to eat? What in the world had happened?

Police Chief Handleman was called. Soon a large crowd—a seething carpet of neighbors, relatives, acquaintances, the concerned, and the curious, swept along in the tide—had swarmed up the cupboards toward the Cochrans' home, where they fanned out and squeezed right up to the line that the doctor had drawn in the dust.

In the pale, milky moonlight, Clarence could recognize Floyd with his fast-talking friends, a group of older, cool-looking guys that Floyd was always trying to impress. They had a slinky way of walking, and they wore the latest caps, molded bits of noodle between their antennae, at a cocky, sideways angle.

"See, I told you!" Floyd kept saying to his friends. "He's a human. You'll believe me now, right?"

Meanwhile, the police chief paced behind the line in the dust and yelled, "Everyone stand back!" The crowd stared at Clarence. Some cried. Someone fainted. Most were appalled and frightened. Never in their long history had anything like this happened among the cockroaches. And never, not even after the Gilmartins' messy Thanksgiving dinners, had the community gathered in such numbers. Everyone seemed to be there, except for a few of the elderly who dozed on the windowsill, and Stephen, who, embarrassed by his youngest brother, must have hidden under the old tea bag on the shelf below.

Squinting, Clarence could make out others beyond the line. Martha McMoffit with all her admirers. Reverend O'Coccus with his head bowed and claws together like a praying mantis. And there, off to the side, stood Willie, as though he didn't know if he was part of the crowd or not. He was staring at Clarence, his eyes wide open and questioning. Beside his feet

was the small dried green pea that, in happier times, they liked to kick back and forth.

"It's me! It's me!" Clarence called out, but Willie looked confused. Soon Willie's mother arrived and hustled him away.

Meanwhile, excited voices cried out from the darkness at the back of the crowd: "Look! There he is!"

"Never mind them," Clarence's mother said to him. She had positioned herself between the crowd and her son, and turned back to her knitting, picking up the ends of two broken toothpicks that she used for needles. "Don't listen. They're all busybodies and gossips right now. You'd think they hadn't a brain in their head, following each other like ants. That's the problem with us roaches sometimes: nobody's got any gumption. Here, let's get you out of view, behind the teapot. They'll all get bored soon enough and leave."

She set down her knitting, scuttled behind him, and, putting her front claws on the rim of the measuring spoon, started pushing him backward. As she pushed, Clarence looked back at the shadowy crowd, trying to find his father's face. Suddenly he heard the soft steps of slippered feet—human feet!—and a gasp rose up from the throng.

Then something extraordinary happened. It was the very thing that elderly cockroaches hissed about when they lectured kids like Clarence on proper cockroach behavior. The Reverend had even described a moment like this in one of his fiery sermons:

From the ceiling came a blaze of pure light.

6 / The Gilmartins

Someone in the crowd cried "Mayday! Scatter!" And of course, Clarence remembered what he'd always been told. As fast as he could, he should run for cover: dive into the nearest crack or under a sponge; squeeze behind a loose baseboard or molding strip; make himself small, tucking in his legs and antennae; stay absolutely still; hold his breath—and not make a sound. He'd always been a pro at scattering.

But to tell the truth, Clarence didn't feel the urge to run just now. He didn't feel like sliding into a dark, dank, narrow space, even if he could have managed it in his new condition. He was oddly comfortable in the spoon, sitting up in the open air, partway behind the teapot where his mother had pushed him. From here, he could see most of the kitchen. And that, in fact, was an amazing thing. As a cockroach, his eyes had only worked in dim light or the dark, but now, as a human boy staring into the blaze of an electric bulb, he could *see*! And as the seconds passed, as his eyes seemed to relax and adjust, he could see *even better*! He saw colors in a way he never had before, great patches of them, and details, too! The bright orange beak of the teapot. The pretty pink and yellow flowers on the wallpaper, woven with green sprigs of fern. The silver wall clock with a face like a crooked smile. The shiny reddish brown of the panicked cockroaches, now a scurrying tangle of antennae, legs, and wings, everyone madly zigzagging across walls and cream-colored cupboards and counters.

Then Clarence saw an upright swath of fuzzy blue come in the doorway. Some kind of coat or bathrobe, he guessed. And wearing it, he knew, was someone he'd heard about but never actually seen. It was Kathryn Gilmartin.

Kathryn Gilmartin was a formidable person. She

entered the kitchen with the patient, determined look of a seventh-grade English teacher, which, in fact, she was. In school, as in grammar, as in raising a child or running a household, she believed there were certain sensible ways of doing things, and these were called "the rules." If you generally worked within them, if you upheld basic standards, she could be easygoing and flexible. She might even overlook obvious violations, like Larry's lazy kitchen cleanup habits, as long as they were corrected in due time. On the other hand—and it was quite some other hand!—if things went beyond a certain point, if things got out of control, she could be tough as nails. Her neck would stiffen. She'd set her jaw. She'd push her hair behind her ears. She'd correct things *in her way*, and there was no changing her mind.

Tonight, as she often did, she'd been up late reading in bed. But tonight, as was *not* her habit, she'd gotten up and walked down to the kitchen for a snack.

Now, when she saw the roaches scattering in the light, she stopped still. Her hand flew up to the base of her neck, and then she made a human sound, a sharp, loud "Oh!"

A few seconds later, another human, Larry Gilmartin, stumbled into the kitchen. Sleep lines creased his face. His sandy hair stood up in some places; in others, it fell into his eyes. His arms groped for the wall and doorframe, and his striped pajama bottoms were twisted. He had the appearance of someone whose parts were flying off in different directions—which was true even when he was wide awake. Although he was a good husband and father, other areas of his life hadn't come together. Once a promising software designer, he'd more recently bounced from one job to another, and after he'd lost his last job, he didn't seem to mind eating breakfast in his pajamas after Kathryn had left early for work. He didn't mind walking Mimi to the elementary school at nine o'clock and walking her home at three-thirty. He didn't mind running errands, buying groceries, returning to the store for things he'd forgotten, and, in one way or another, getting dinner on the table when Kathryn came home.

Clarence watched all this from his spoon beside the teapot. He saw Larry, like someone emerging from a nightmare, blinking in the bright kitchen. *"What? What is it? Is everybody all right?"*

"Cockroaches!" Kathryn said. "Look!"

"Where?" Larry looked all around, scrunching up his face to see.

"You missed them. There were hundreds!"

Clarence heard a girl's voice call from down the hall, "Mommy? Daddy? What's going on?"

Kathryn answered in a calmer tone. "We're right here, sweetie. Go back to bed. It's nothing."

But the girl, Mimi, strode into the kitchen in a huge white T-shirt that hung down to her knees. She wore her red hair pulled back in a frizzy ponytail. Along the edge of her scalp some short strands stuck out and made Clarence think of electrified wires. By now, she apparently knew that when adults say "it's nothing," it's usually something important.

"I heard someone scream," she said.

"Mommy thinks she saw some bugs," Larry explained.

"What kind?"

"We're not sure."

"I think they're cockroaches," Kathryn said.

Mimi nodded. "Interesting," she said.

Mimi Gilmartin was ten years old, a beginning fifth-grader with a particularly active mind. She was interested in *everything*. Some kids called her a "know-it-all." Often she baffled her own parents. At home, she'd taught herself calligraphy, the Greek alphabet, and Roman history, and every night she wrote in a "journal," crammed with her important ideas. She'd never call it a mere "diary." At school, she was in the advanced math and science groups. She took certain issues very seriously. On an information sheet for the school nurse, where she'd noted her allergies to bee stings and cat hair, she'd listed her "Other Concerns" as "world peace, global warming, and endangered species—including human beings!" In class, she'd wave her hand wildly with a question that, in her excitement, she'd sometimes forget when she was called on. Now, though, she hadn't forgotten what she was dying to know: "How many legs did they have?"

"What? The cockroaches? I couldn't *count* their legs," her mother answered. "Does it matter?"

"Of course! Cockroaches have six legs. Spiders have eight and no antennae. How about wings? Cockroaches can't usually fly, but did you see wings?" Mimi asked.

"I can't be sure. I think they had wings."

"How many pair?"

"Oh, come on!"

"Cockroaches have one pair. Beetles have two—a set of outside wings, like shields, that protect their fragile inside ones. Isn't that interesting?"

"Fascinating!" Larry said. "But not at this hour. It's the middle of the night. Get back to bed."

"You know, if they're cockroaches," Mimi went right on, "they're incredibly adaptable. There are thousands of species. They've been on this planet forever, long before humans, and they'll still be here when we're gone."

"Go!" Larry said, raising his voice.

And so she left the kitchen, but not before saying that it wasn't fair, that her parents were "stifling" her "natural curiosity."

Even from his spoon high on the shelf, Clarence could see that Mimi's eyes were almost a neon blue, and that freckles the size of pinpoints covered her nose, which he thought looked proud yet delicate. He watched her move toward the door with her head held high. Something about her held his gaze. *This is an interesting human,* he thought.

7 / Down the Drain

They're clever, the little buggers," Kathryn said to Larry when Mimi had left for her bedroom. "Not a one in sight now."

In fact, from the measuring spoon on the top shelf, Clarence saw that the roaches *had* all disappeared. The whole kitchen was still and quiet, but alive with listening and fear.

"You're sure you saw them?" Larry whispered, as if there was something so strange about the night that he had to lower his voice.

"Yes, of course I saw them," Kathryn replied. "I'd just come in here to get a snack. They were scurrying all around!" She glanced at the stove top and counters. "What a mess! No wonder we have roaches!"

With her slippers barely making a sound, she moved toward the sink and counter, where the remains of the Chinese takeout were piled. She stopped and listened. She lifted one of the cardboard cartons, but amazingly no roach was underneath. She picked up an uneaten fortune cookie, turned it in her hand, then shook it hard, the way you'd shake a bottle of ketchup. Yet no roach fell out.

Then, tightening the belt of her bathrobe, bending close and pushing back her hair, she peered at a spoon lying in the watery glop in the sink. "You don't believe me?" she said quietly to Larry. "Watch this." With her finger, she pressed down on the large end of the spoon, which made the other end rise up like a seesaw.

And huddled there beneath it, with his antennae tight around his sides, was Clarence's friend Willie—small, alone, and exposed. Clarence, in his own spoon high above, caught his breath. He was about to cry "Look out!" but before he did, Willie shot into action, scrambled over logjams of chopsticks, slid down a slick noodle, and, using all his momentum, took a desperate, flying leap—and disappeared down the drain into the garbage disposal.

"Did you see that?" Kathryn asked.

"I did," Larry said.

Then Kathryn did an astonishing, and, to Clarence, an altogether *inhuman* thing. He could see it with his eyes and hear it with his ears, but his mind just wouldn't accept it. She turned on the faucet and, at the switch by the window, flicked on the disposal. It made that familiar grinding, chewing sound, and then it purred smoothly.

What has she done?

"That's just the tip of the iceberg," she said, turning off the switch. The disposal went quiet. "Now we need to deal with the rest of them."

"But not tonight," Larry replied gently. He put his hand on her arm. "Look at the time."

And indeed, if they had looked closely at the clock, not only would they have learned that it was after midnight, but they might have seen Floyd, still trying to impress his friends, boldly hiding behind the minute hand.

"You wanted a snack?" Larry asked. Using his hand like a plow, he began clearing a space at the kitchen table, pushing aside plastic packets of soy sauce, a Scotch Tape dispenser, the salt and pepper shakers, a stubby pencil, and a pad of paper.

"I seem to have lost my appetite," Kathryn replied. She moved toward the door, then paused for a second, glancing back toward the cupboards and counters where she'd seen the scattering roaches. She switched off the light. "We'll deal with them tomorrow," she said.

8 / Morning Prayers

It took a full hour before anyone moved, except for Floyd, who peeked out from behind the minute hand. The kitchen, so alive with activity not long before, seemed frozen in shock and horror. Then, one by one, antennae emerged from cracks, cabinets, drawers, and the vents in various appliances. Heads, thoraxes, abdomens, and wings followed. Knee by knee, Clarence's mother rose from where she crouched on the top shelf. With bits of scrambled egg on the barbs of his front legs, his father poked out of the fried rice on the counter. Dr. Blatt had to be rescued from the curve of an extra-wide flexible straw where he'd gotten himself stuck. And then, lo and behold, Willie, who must have clung to the inner wall of the disposal, crawled from the drain, looking dazed and dizzy, his antennae twisted like pretzels.

Soon the community tiptoed in shadows toward the corner cabinet, where the Gilmartins kept their canned and packaged goods. This was where Clarence, when his mother insisted, had always gone to church. It was where Reverend O'Coccus, inspired by a radio program he heard from a neighboring apartment, wore himself out on Sunday evenings, preaching from the top of a can of clam chowder. And it was where now almost everyone assembled.

While he couldn't see the proceedings from his spoon on the top shelf, Clarence could listen to them. He recognized the grave and trembling voice of the Reverend, who reminded the community that "from this very pulpit" he had warned of a fiery light, a sign of things to come, unless "some of those among us mend their ways—and quick!"

Then, evidently, Mayor Grimes went to the pulpit to speak of more practical matters. He declared a Code Red Alert. Everyone must be extremely cautious. Under no circumstances should anyone be seen by the Gilmartins. All nymphs must be accompanied by parents. Beginning at four-thirty each morning, a curfew would be imposed. No one should venture from their cracks and crevices, or there would be a price to pay.

Now the Reverend spoke again. He recited the Twenty-third Psalm: "The Lord is my shepherd; I shall not want . . ." And promising to live "in the house of the Lord"—as well as that of the Gilmartins—forever, everyone scuttled home.

It is interesting how danger—real, gut-wrenching, fear-for-your-life danger—can encourage a more co-operative attitude, even among certain young males. Back home, Floyd and Stephen, with only mild complaints, went about the job of preparing their new sleeping places on the lower shelf above the stove, since the top shelf was now off-limits. Stephen, bringing along his favorite possession—an aluminum foil mirror—would hole up in the loose spine of *The Fannie Farmer Cookbook*. Floyd arranged a comfortable place for himself in an empty Hershey bar wrapper. As always, Clarence's father would sleep in the unused recipe box, between the 3 × 5 file card for chocolate cheesecake and the one for Swedish meatballs. Unfortunately, he wouldn't be snuggling there with Clarence's mother—because, of course, she was quarantined.

At the moment, she could be seen on the top shelf, once again carrying Clarence on her back. She had taken him from the measuring spoon, then up the winged side of the bird-shaped teapot, around its rim, into the long tunnel of its throat, and out near the hole at the end of its beak. That's where Clarence would bed down for the day, in Stephen's old sleeping spot. His mother, in turn, would sleep in Floyd's old nest beneath the candlesnuffer, where she would be close to Clarence.

As she tucked Clarence in with a bit of calico cloth for a blanket, he asked, "Am I ever going to get better?"

"Sure. Soon you'll be back to normal."

"Then why has this happened? Why have I changed? Was it something I did?"

She looped her antennae around his narrow shoulders, hugging him long and hard. "No. Of course not. It's nobody's fault."

"Then *why*?"

"I don't know," she said after thinking a moment. "But there must be a good reason."

Soon she listened to Clarence's prayers, which she said were especially important now, "when we all might be in danger."

Aloud, he asked God to bless and protect the entire community, and by name he prayed for his aunts, uncles, cousins . . . and his parents . . . and Willie, of course.

"And . . . ?" his mother prodded.

"And Willie's little sister Midge."

"And . . . ?"

"The Gilmartins. Bless them. And help them to be nice to us."

"Yes. And . . . ?"

"Sparky," he said. Sparky was the Gilmartins' dog.

"And . . . ?"

"Who else is there?"

She let out a sigh. "What about your *brothers*?" Then, for about the millionth time, she said that Stephen—sometimes selfishly, she had to admit—was "growing into adulthood" and that Floyd, for all his tough-guy bluster, was really "just a softy inside."

Clarence let out a sigh of his own. "All right," he said at last. "God bless my brothers, too."

9 / The Motel

After his mother had kissed him, said "See you in the evening," and left, Clarence closed his eyes. Yet how could he sleep? Never before had this been a problem. He'd lie down and think of kicking that dried pea with Willie. Back and forth . . . Back and forth . . .

Then the next thing you knew, he'd be sound asleep, and then it would be evening again, and Clarence would be wide awake, ready for an adventure.

But on that following night, a Monday, the second evening since he'd changed into a boy, Clarence's mother had to jostle him awake. All day, he'd had trouble sleeping. The light had kept waking him and filling him with strange excitement. From the beak of the teapot, he'd watched it. It began as a glow, then a bright curve on top of the building beyond the courtyard. It rose and grew, reminding him of the moon, but this was so much bigger and brighter! It grew until it was whole and round and so bright that he couldn't look straight at it. It poured through the window in thick shafts, dancing on the long neck of the faucet, filling the kitchen with a lemony color and a warmth that tingled on his skin and spread to the very heart of him. It was wonderful!

Now, when it was getting dark and he'd usually be getting up, all he wanted was to lie down again. The darkness made him drowsy. Still, his mother looked at him in her encouraging way and said, "We can't let this quarantine get us down. A short stroll might do you some good. Food will help, too. I bet you're hungry."

She was more right about this than she could have imagined. Last night's gloppy sweet-and-sour sauce that Stephen had brought up to them before the crowd had gathered just hadn't appealed to Clarence. He could only eat a little of it, as well as some crumbs from a stale saltine. Underneath that single hole in the middle of his abdomen, he was feeling sharp pangs, and his head was getting fuzzy. He had the sense that in his new condition he was more fragile and finicky about food—and less able to withstand discomfort.

"Let's see what your brothers and father are up to," his mother continued. "I wonder what delicious treats the Gilmartins have left out tonight."

As she tenderly supported him under his elbow, he crawled on his knees and the weird ends of his front legs back through the throat of the teapot and along the rim. She skidded him down the bird's wing, and they moved past the old ball of string to the line in the dust along the edge of the shelf, where they looked out on the kitchen. It was bathed in moonlight again. Due to the Red Alert, caution filled the air. Below, small groups huddled on the stove, everyone glancing over their shoulders. No kids swung on the lamp's pull-string, and no couples strolled under the radiator.

Yet something else was also different. Clarence saw his father and brothers on the counter, but tonight they were moving oddly, wandering aimlessly, as if they were stunned and perplexed.

Then Clarence saw—or he *didn't* see—what must have perplexed them. It jarred him wide awake. *Where are all the food-slathered dishes and utensils? Where are all the spills and splatters?*

Amazingly, the counter and stove top were spotless. The garbage was sealed in a plastic bag beside the dishwasher. The sink gleamed! Sparky's bowl was washed and upturned on a clean towel. A top was on the sugar bowl. The table was neat. Not even a crumb on the floor!

"What's happened?" Clarence gasped.

For a moment, his mother, horrified, didn't say anything. Then she said, "The Gilmartins—they must have cleaned up after dinner!"

Clarence was shocked. How would everyone eat? But he was also surprised, when he thought about it, that he could understand why the Gilmartins might want to clean up the kitchen. The stink and mess of dirty dishes! And you had to admit: there was something beautiful about a scoured sink, like a shining bowl of moonlight.

Then Clarence saw—and this time he *did* see—another thing that was perplexing. Behind the sink, where the counter met the backsplash, a cardboard box lay on its side. It was about three inches long, an inch wide, and an inch tall. Its visible end was open, and a gently sloping ramp led invitingly into its dark interior. From a distance, it looked like a nice, cozy place to make a home.

"What's that?" he asked his mother.

"I haven't the foggiest," she said.

He peered down at the box, and on its side he saw some marks he'd never seen before. They looked like this:

ROACH MOTEL

Squinting hard, his eyes moved from the R to the O and pretty soon to the H. They leaped through midair to get to the M, and eventually they reached the E and the L. Then the marks made clearer sounds in Clarence's head than he'd ever heard before! They were words! He was *reading* them! And the words said, *Roach Motel*.

"Mom, what's a motel?"

"It's a place to sleep when you're traveling," she said. "I've heard they're often sleazy."

"What's it doing *here*?"

"I don't know—if that's what it is. It seems fishy to me."

Just then Clarence saw his father and brothers, who'd spotted the motel, approaching it with great curiosity. He could tell by the way their antennae were stretching and sniffing that the motel was giving off some wonderful odor. Perhaps something rotted was inside. It seemed to be calling to them, and the closer they got—lightly touching its sides, corners, and that ramp leading into the dark opening—the more interested they became. On Stephen, Clarence noticed, the motel had the same wing-shivering effect as Martha McMoffit when she walked beside him. For Floyd, was it just something new and cool? And you might have thought that their father had caught a whiff of a double-cheese, sausage, and pepperoni pizza. They were all spellbound.

That's when Clarence saw Reverend O'Coccus moving resolutely toward them. The Reverend stepped between the motel and Clarence's father and brothers. He stood on the edge of the ramp on his hind and middle legs. He held one front leg out straight like the police chief saying Stop. "Lead us not into temptation!" he said.

For Clarence's father, that seemed to break the spell. He stopped, shook himself, and, taking each of his older sons by an elbow, backed softly away from the motel,

the way you'd
retreat from a snake
or centipede. He
thanked the Reverend for coming
to the rescue.
When they'd
backed up a safe

distance, Clarence heard his father say, "Phew, that was close! I don't know what got into me."

"But did you smell that?" Stephen said, his eyes wide, his wings still vibrating. "So scrumptious! Like all the spoiled fruit in the world!" He kept looking back at the motel. "Oh, it hurts just to think about it!"

"Let's go home," their father said. "Not a word about this to your mother. Thank goodness she wasn't here to see. We'd be in *big* trouble with her!"

"That's right!" Clarence's mother called down to her husband. Along with Clarence, she'd been watching everything from the top shelf. Then she said, "And you, Stephen—especially you. I know you've got a mind of your own, but you stay away from that motel. Hear me?"

10 / A Mother's Advice

From friend to friend and neighbor to neighbor, news got around quickly: the Gilmartins had cleaned their kitchen, and a suspicious motel that smelled heavenly had appeared behind the sink. In an emergency meeting, the cockroach Town Council met in the "miscellaneous drawer," where the Gilmartins tossed everything from loose flashlight batteries to scissors to playing cards to corn holders. The Council approved the mayor's Red Alert, declared the motel off-limits, and instructed the Parks Department to contact a friendly spider about building a fence of sticky cobwebs around it.

Food would have to be saved. A special committee

would make a list of the town's extra stale crackers and see if other apartments in the building were available, in case the roach community had to leave. Finally, the mayor encouraged everyone, while observing the Red Alert, to conduct their lives as calmly as possible and in a spirit of cooperation and good cheer.

A couple hours later, Dr. Blatt visited Clarence, who was resting again in the measuring spoon. Accompanying him was Dr. Spry, a special doctor who called himself a "psychologist." As Clarence's mother stood by nervously, Dr. Spry asked Clarence some questions, like "Have you ever felt this way before?" He unrolled a photograph, somewhat larger than a postage stamp, that must have been cut from a human magazine. It showed a thick, uncooked, rancid-looking lamb chop, surrounded by a gooey rind of yellow fat and a swarm of flies. "This should stir something inside you," he explained. He asked Clarence to study the photo as often as he could, especially before mealtime. It was supposed to make him hungry and feel like his old self again.

But mostly it made Clarence feel sick. He could barely stand to look at it.

An hour after that, another doctor called a "physical therapist" arrived. Her name was Veronica. With her, she brought an orange bead, about the size of a marble. Using her considerable bulk and strength, she got Clarence out of the spoon and draped him over the bead with his stomach down, so just his "hands"— that's what she called them—and his feet touched the shelf. "No more crawling like a human baby," she said. "No more crawling on your knees. Keep your thorax and abdomen up! Crawl on the *ends* of *all* your legs! That's how we do it!" Three times each day Clarence was to practice his "bead exercises." They would build up his muscles and help him move properly, so he could scoot and skedaddle just like a roach again.

But mostly the exercises made him feel sore.

"I think I'd like to try something else," Clarence said to his mother after the doctors had all gone. He felt an odd restlessness spreading throughout his body, especially to his legs.

"What do you have in mind?" his mother asked in a hesitant tone.

"I'm not sure," he said, "but I feel like there's something I have to do."

As if listening to a voice within, he got himself into a kneeling position beside the measuring spoon. With both hands, he grasped the rim. Then, little by little, unbending his legs, he rose up higher and higher, higher than he'd ever been before, his whole body nearly straight and vertical!

With his head so high, he swayed dizzily for a moment, so he had to hold on tight to the rim. The shelf and his feet seemed very far away, and his mother, who was tilting her head to look up at his face, was way down there, too.

"You're so . . . *tall!*" she said with a mixture of awe and alarm. Then, after another minute, she said, "How will I hug you when you're way up there?"

He didn't have an answer for this. He felt all strange and giddy. No roach had ever stood so high. His head, like a turret, was on top of his neck . . . which was on top of his shoulders . . . which were on top of his chest . . . which was on top of his waist . . . which was on top of his legs . . . which were on top of his distant feet. Everything was neatly stacked. When he twisted his neck, he could see almost all the way around. From way up here, the world looked so much wider—and his mother so much smaller.

Now he let go of the rim of the spoon with one hand, and then let go with the other. For the first time in his life, he was on his own two legs, teetering but not falling, with his arms straight out, awkwardly balancing himself. It was scary, but he was doing it! He was *standing*, his feet apart, his chest pushed forward, his shoulders square. He was an upright creature!

But that wasn't all he did. Still balancing and focusing all his attention, he lifted his right leg at the hip, bent his knee, and swung his foot forward, landing on his heel. Lurching, his body came right along—amazingly, still upright!—and as it did, his other leg lifted at the hip, the knee bent, and *that* foot swung forward and landed farther ahead of the first. Now the right leg repeated what it had just accomplished. Then the left again. Right. Left. Right. Left. In this way, Clarence propelled his body three or four inches across the shelf. "Look, Mom, I'm *walking*!"

He walked around the measuring spoon and around the teapot and the candlesnuffer. Then, for a challenge, he walked around them all in the other direction. It was fascinating and thrilling how he could do this, and, as he kept at it, he walked more smoothly. He didn't need to hold out his arms for balance anymore. They fell and dangled at his sides. He could use them for other things!

What a way to travel! How dignified and uplifting! How pleased he was with his legs striding, his head held high, and his arms swinging loose and free!

Back at the measuring spoon, he looked down at his mother.

"I don't think this is going according to doctor's orders," she said, her voice quavering. Her face seemed pained yet proud. "You may not be recovering your old self, but I *do* believe you're getting better."

All at once Clarence felt bad that he was standing high above his mother, and so she wouldn't have to talk *up* to him like this, he got back down on his hands and knees, where he was face-to-face with her again.

From the spoon, she picked up the photo that Dr. Spry had left. She held it unrolled in her front claws. Then, very deliberately, she tore it into tiny pieces and let them flutter down. She rolled the orange bead behind the teapot. "Let's forget about these," she said. "Let's forget about what the doctors want you to be—and even what *I* might want you to be." With tears rimming her eyes, she looked into his, and he could tell that, more than anything else in the world, she loved what she saw when he was happy.

"Be who you are," she said. "Listen to your heart, let your life follow, and you will do wonderful things. Go ahead, Clarence, stand and walk."

11 / A Sad Event

It was just after the curfew had gone into effect that night—in the predawn dark of the morning. The kitchen was quiet and empty, everyone having retired to their cracks and crannies and bedded down for the day. In the beak of the teapot, Clarence was lying on his stomach on the calico cloth. He was nibbling on a piece of stale saltine when he saw something moving near the sink.

Clarence recognized him by his stocky, beetley shape, his slinky walk, and by the silhouette of the cap, tilted sideways on his head. It was Floyd. Just behind him crept three of his older friends in single file, along the seam at the bottom of the backsplash.

Together they stopped at the cobweb fence that surrounded the Roach Motel. The others gathered around Floyd and patted him on his wings. For a second, Floyd hesitated as if he had a twinge of doubt. And then, before Clarence could figure out what was going on, two of Floyd's friends lifted the bottom strand of the fence and Floyd scooted under it, his cap snagging on the cobweb. In an instant, he was standing at the top of the ramp to the motel. He looked so proud. He glanced back to see that his friends were watching him. Then he disappeared inside.

Clarence would never forget what happened—or didn't happen—next. For a minute, two minutes, three minutes, Floyd's friends didn't move. Like Clarence, they just looked at the dark opening at the top of the ramp where Floyd had disappeared, the way you'd look at a stage where a curtain was about to rise. Only no curtain rose. No one reappeared on the ramp, and the longer Clarence watched and waited, the more it seemed to him that something just *had* to happen.

And yet nothing happened. There wasn't even a sound—what a silence!—until Clarence heard the nervous whispering of one of Floyd's friends: "Psst. Floyd, you can come out now. You've made your point."

But nothing happened.

"Hey, dude, if you don't come out, we're gettin' outta here anyway."

Still nothing happened.

A few more minutes passed, and then Floyd's friends fled. They left nothing behind—except for Floyd's cap hanging on the fence.

That's what Clarence was staring at, when, without his even noticing it, the dawn streamed through the window. That's what he was *still* staring at, when, around seven o'clock, Kathryn Gilmartin, dressed in a beige sweater and crisply ironed navy blue pants, walked into the kitchen. Going straight to the sink, she picked up the Roach Motel and peered into the opening at the end of the ramp.

"Just one?" she said aloud. A wave of disappointment crossed her face, and, as if it were an eggshell or an apple core, she dropped the motel into a fresh plastic trash bag which she knotted at the top. With the bag, she went into the living room and turned toward the apartment door. Clarence heard her slide the safety chain and unlock the dead bolt. He heard the door squeak open as she took the bag out into the world, probably to a garbage chute. When she returned, without the bag, she was carrying a newspaper which she set on the table. From a package in a drawer beside the stove, she unwrapped a brand-new Roach Motel and placed it where the old one had been.

Now she washed her hands beneath the faucet. *How can she be so calm?* Clarence thought. She fixed her breakfast, ate while reading the paper, then made

Mimi's bag lunch, as she must have done on thousands of school-day mornings. She cleaned up her dishes and utensils. From outside came the familiar rumble of a garbage truck pulling to a stop, then that high-pitched *rrrr . . . rrrr* as it squeezed trash into its belly. At the table, Kathryn picked up her canvas satchel that sprouted with folders and papers. She walked out of the kitchen. The apartment door opened and closed. The lock clicked, and the kitchen, bathed in lemony morning light, was silent and still again.

12 / All Alone

Even though Floyd had been something less than a perfect citizen, his disappearance and death in the Roach Motel deeply affected the entire community. Almost everyone attended the memorial service the following night, when Floyd was remembered for his "youthful energy." The next night, almost everyone came to the second emergency Town Council meeting, where the special committee reported additional alarming news. While the extra stale crackers would hold out for a few more days, there were *no* other available apartments in the rest of the building. Every other kitchen was overcrowded. Water was scarce on the fourth and sixth floors, and food riots had erupted in apartment #539. So the Gilmartins' kitchen was it. Should famine result from the Gilmartins' new housecleaning practices, and should the community have to leave, there was no safe place to go *to*.

Missing from the meeting and even the memorial service were Clarence and his mother, who were still under quarantine on the top shelf, overcome with grief and guilt.

I could have stopped it! Clarence kept saying to himself. *I could have seen the trouble Floyd was getting into—it was just like him. I could have yelled NO! when he was on the ramp. I should have done SOMETHING!*

Instead, he'd just watched, dumbfounded.

"I saw it all," Clarence, weeping, had confessed to his parents. "I saw him standing there. I saw him go into the motel. Then I didn't see him anymore."

When he'd said this, all the light went out of his mother's face. "Say that again," she'd said in a dead voice he didn't recognize.

So he'd told them again.

Then she'd turned away and crawled beneath the bell of the candlesnuffer. She refused to come out. From the edge of the shelf, Clarence's father called to her and coaxed her, but to no avail. Dr. Spry paid a visit, but with no better result. Standing outside the candlesnuffer, Clarence heard her wailing over and over in there, "Floyd. My son. Where are you?"

And all Clarence could think of to say was, "It's me. Clarence. I'm sorry."

But she'd wailed even louder. "I love you," she'd managed to say to him, gasping. Still, she wouldn't come out.

Meanwhile, Clarence's father grew enraged, working himself into a state, ranting and raving on the bottom shelf to anyone who might be listening. How could this have happened? How could you explain it? He didn't mean to blame Clarence, but wasn't it strange—was it just a coincidence?—that *all* these horrible things were happening after Clarence had turned into a human? That blaze of light in the kitchen. The cleaned stove and countertops. The motel. And now Floyd dead and gone. Not even a body! Nothing to hold, nothing of *him*, except for this measly cap. And what might happen next?

The world, his father went on bitterly, was a terrible place. Nothing was fair. Everything was rigged in favor of humans, and now one of his sons was one of *them*, while another had died at their hands. Hadn't he warned everyone about the Gilmartins? The "whole lot of them" were evil and murderous. They were *animals*! He, for one, would get back at them. He'd soil their clean dishes and utensils. He'd give them diseases like salmonella, gastroenteritis, giardia, strep and staph infections, and explosive diarrhea. Nothing would stop him. He'd do it, he promised. If he could, he'd give every one of them the plague!

Overhearing this, Clarence put his hands over his ears—he felt sad, horrified, and ashamed—but he couldn't block out his father's raging.

It seemed like Stephen couldn't stand it either. After the memorial service, he didn't come home. He stayed out night and day, not even taking his preening gel or mirror. Their father looked for him but couldn't find him, and no one, not even Martha Mc-Moffit, could say where he'd gone.

So Clarence was alone. His father wouldn't speak to him. All night Clarence stood beside the candle-snuffer, while his mother gasped and wailed, her sounds ringing around in the bell. Finally, near dawn, her moaning turned into restless, whimpering sleep, and he made his way back to the beak of the teapot, where he seemed like the only creature awake in the world. He said his prayers now without his mother listening, and he wondered if God might not be listening either. Still, he prayed that his mother would come out from under the candlesnuffer and wrap her antennae around his shoulders. He prayed that his father wouldn't be so mad. He prayed that Stephen would come home and that Floyd was up there with the angels, with wings that might actually fly.

Then he also prayed that he might get better and change back into a cockroach. This being a human was confusing and difficult. It made him feel like a freak. His father was right: horrible things were certainly happening. And maybe, somehow, they *were*

Clarence's fault; surely other roaches were thinking the same thing, too. He wasn't even a curiosity anymore. No one except the doctors came near the top shelf. Not even Willie would acknowledge him. When they saw each other from a distance, Willie turned away in embarrassment and continued kicking the dried pea with some roach Clarence had never seen before.

Still praying, Clarence promised to do his nightly exercises on the orange bead. He didn't want to stand on two feet anymore. He wanted to dash around on his old six legs.

Then after he'd said "amen," he tried in his mind to put back together the photograph of the lamb chop with the gooey rind and the swarm of flies. He wanted spoiled food to make his mouth water and get him all excited again. *Why can't I be who I used to be? Why can't I be like everyone else?*

But just thinking of that picture still made him feel sick, and, unable to fall asleep, he cried silently into his hands.

13 / The Phone Call

Could things get any worse than this for Clarence? I'm afraid they did.

His father was true to his grim promise. On the night after the memorial service, while almost everyone was at the Council meeting, he sneaked away and purposely left his sticky droppings, crawling with germs, on a spoon in the silverware drawer instead of in one of the special "waste areas" in the backs of certain cupboards. He must have figured that Kathryn would be the first to use the spoon. With it, she'd eat her morning cereal, and the droppings would make her good and sick. If things worked out the way he wanted, they might even kill her.

Instead, it was Mimi who used the spoon the next

day. Then, sick to her stomach, she came home from school before noon. For an hour, Clarence heard her heaving and hacking in the bathroom. It sounded like all Mimi's insides had come out, and still she kept throwing up. Even in the midst of his own sadness, Clarence felt sorry for her.

Soon, Kathryn rushed home from work. She and Larry spoke in anxious voices:

"She's so pale!"

"So weak! She's getting worse!"

"What on earth could it be?"

Kathryn called their doctor and the rescue squad, and soon the apartment was a frenzy of clattering equipment, urgent questions, and heavy feet clomping around. Then the next thing you know, the apartment was empty of humans, not a sound, except for the dwindling pulse of a siren speeding farther and farther away.

None of the Gilmartins came back that afternoon, that evening, or that night. Sparky, their dog, lumbered into the kitchen a few times, looked around, whined, and nudged his empty food bowl. The roach community, already stunned and reeling, seemed to sense that something else was very wrong. Clarence's father stayed on the lower shelf and out of sight. In a hastily arranged meeting in the corner cabinet, Reverend O'Coccus offered prayers for the sick, prayers of repentance, and prayers for help in time of trouble. Mayor Grimes pleaded for calm.

Nothing made sense to Clarence anymore. How could Kathryn have turned on them? And how could his own father have done such a terrible thing in revenge?

Then, about nine o'clock the next morning, a Friday, the apartment door opened, and Clarence heard the voices of *all three* of the Gilmartins. Though Mimi's voice seemed shaky, she was home again! He heard her walk down the hall, accompanied by her parents, who must have gotten her into bed. Then Kathryn and Larry, still in yesterday's rumpled clothes, came into the kitchen.

"Food poisoning?" Larry said. "But neither of us got sick. What could have caused it?"

"I think I know," Kathryn replied, as she got a ginger ale from the fridge and fixed a tray for Mimi.

"What?"

"Those roaches. I'd bet my life on it. We're lucky it was a mild case."

When she returned to the kitchen, Larry had taken Sparky outside, and Clarence could see that Kathryn's jaw was set. She went straight to the sink and picked up the Roach Motel, which no roaches had dared go near after what had happened to Floyd. She peered inside it and said, "Enough is enough! This isn't working. We're not taking any more chances!"

From the cupboard beside the fridge, she pulled out the Yellow Pages, then pressed the buttons on the phone. She waited a few seconds, listening. Then she said, "I could use your help with a problem."

There was a pause, after which she replied, "Roaches." Then there were more pauses and comments.

"Yes, it's a current problem . . .

"Yes, I'd say an infestation. A couple hundred, at least . . .

"Just in the kitchen . . .

"The customized treatment plan—does it kill them in all the cracks and crevices? . . .

"It's Kathryn, with a K and a Y and no E on the end. Gilmartin is the last name. 902 23rd St., Wyndam Court Apartments, apartment #518 . . .

"Yes. A dog. Is that a problem? . . .

"Good. How soon can you come? . . .

"Tomorrow? You work on Saturday? First thing in the morning? Eight o'clock? . . .

"Great. See you then."

Clarence watched as she put the phone back in its cradle. The word "exterminator" suddenly came to his mind, a word he'd only heard whispered in stories told by visitors from far away in the building. In the stories, an exterminator was described as standing erect on two very tall legs, and wearing a white uniform, a white cap, and goggles that made him look like an insect, though he didn't fool anyone. Instead of wings, he carried on his back a canister of deadly liquid and in one hand a wand that sprayed the liquid everywhere. No one survived.

Never, so far as Clarence knew, had an exterminator set foot in the Gilmartins' apartment. For him, an exterminator seemed make-believe, like a monster in a fairy tale. But as he kept thinking about what he'd just heard, there was no getting around it. Kathryn had called an exterminator—a real one. And tomorrow morning he'd be here.

14 / Over the Edge

During the rest of that Friday, Mimi got better and better. By midmorning, she was sipping chicken broth at the kitchen table. By noon, she was dressed and wolfing down eggs and toast, and by late afternoon, Clarence heard her on the phone with a classmate, finding out what she'd missed in school.

If nothing else had been on his mind, this would have cheered Clarence. But alone with his terrible knowledge of what was about to happen, he couldn't feel anything except despair. He'd spent most of that Friday in a daze, dozing and looking out from his bed in the beak of the teapot as the sky changed in the window. At one point, he saw Larry come in with grocery bags, one of which he spilled on the floor. At another point, Mimi fed Sparky, and now, as sunlight faded on the building across the courtyard, all three of the Gilmartins sat around the table with a box of pizza in the middle.

They were talking and eating at the same time in that way humans do. Clarence could see the frizzy electric strands that had popped up along Mimi's hairline, and there was that quick, insistent way that she moved her head, her ponytail bobbing, when she had something important to say—which was often. This evening she was holding forth on the fate of the yellow-crowned night herons, birds whose homes in lowland forests were being wiped out by lumber companies and developers. This, she said, was "an outrage," and if she was ever in charge of things, "it would *never* happen!"

Mightn't the issue be a little more complicated? Larry asked gently. Weren't the developers providing homes for another species, namely human beings?

But Mimi would have none of it. Before they cut down a single tree, the developers should have thought about the health of the planet, by which she meant "every living thing!"

Clarence liked this about Mimi. She took herself

seriously. She seemed so grown-up. She made her views known, and she didn't back down. Just listening to her voice and seeing her hair, her freckles, and her bright blue eyes perked him up a bit.

Having expressed her views on the yellow-crowned night herons, Mimi then launched into the "crisis of the coral reefs," followed by a spirited discussion of the meatpacking industry. Were her parents aware of how many innocent animals were killed every day in the stockyards? This, she said, was another outrage, and that was why, right there and then, she was announcing that she was not eating the pepperoni on her pizza. That was why she'd been stacking the round slices neatly on the side of her plate and sopping up all the "animal fat" with her paper napkin!

Knowing very well the taste of pepperoni and its sweet, spicy grease, Clarence was astounded. Here was a person who acted on her beliefs. Here was a person with *gumption*! He remembered what his mother had said about that, and he remembered what she'd said about listening to his heart and standing up and walking.

Now Mimi's example and his mother's words filled him with admiration. Slowly, a kind of desperate courage rose up alongside his sadness. Shouldn't a healthy planet include cockroaches, who are among its oldest citizens? Why should Mimi's family sit here eating pizza, while his—what remained of it—would soon be exterminated? Shouldn't *his* community be respected? Why should cockroaches die?

He stood—too quickly—and hit his head on the roof of the ceramic bird's beak, but it didn't shake his determination. He would try to do something about this situation. He'd do everything humanly possible. If help wouldn't be coming to him, then he'd just have to go out and get it.

While he was thinking and feeling all this, the Gilmartins had finished their pizza and cleaned up every crumb in the kitchen. The window had darkened. Kathryn had turned off the table lamp. The flickering light of a television came through the doorway that led to the living room, and Clarence could imagine Larry sinking deeper into a lounge chair. Kathryn went off to the study to pay bills. Mimi headed to her room to do homework. Eventually, Larry took the dog for a walk, called good night to Mimi, and went to bed. Soon Kathryn followed.

Crouching in the beak of the teapot, Clarence heard water running in the bathroom as Mimi took a shower and brushed her teeth. Moments later, her steps went back down the hall, and her bedroom door shut. *Maybe if I can just talk with her,* he thought, *if I can just tell her what's happening to us, maybe she'll help us out.*

On hands and knees, Clarence moved down the throat of the teapot and carefully around the rim. He slid down the wing. It was ten-fifteen by the clock on the wall, and he knew that he had just fifteen minutes before the roach community in the kitchen would wake up. He heard no moans from the bell of the candlesnuffer. No raging from the shelf below. In the building across the courtyard, some lights winked out. His eyes fell on the ball of string nearby. Then he looked at his hands with their stubby fingers, and a plan took shape in his mind.

True, he couldn't climb walls anymore, and he couldn't walk upside down on the ceiling. But he had eight strong fingers and two stout thumbs, the combination of which seemed cleverly designed for grasping, twisting, and tying knots. Moreover, he had a head like a hive on top of his shoulders, and in it swarmed all kinds of ideas! In it buzzed *ingenuity*!

The ball of string was twice as tall as Clarence, yet he managed to roll it forward, until he'd unraveled about eight inches. With the loose end, he fashioned a lasso which he swung in a circle above his head. On his first try, he threw it over the neck of the teapot, like a cowboy roping a mustang. He pulled it snug.

The teapot didn't budge. He dropped the string and pushed the ball toward the edge the shelf. Then,

after a mighty *umph*, he watched it roll off and disappear. He heard it unwind as it fell through the air, until it made a soft, satisfying *phlunk* when it hit the kitchen floor.

Now Clarence went over to the grove of wineglasses and found something that he remembered from when he and Willie used to kick the pea back and forth—a narrow, curved shard of glass, a chip about a quarter-inch long. Along one side it was sharp; along the other it was rounded. *This will come in handy,* he figured, since he didn't have his claws for cutting things. He picked it up carefully, as you'd pick up a knife, then returned to the teapot and followed the string to the line in the dust that Dr. Blatt had drawn along the edge.

The line seemed like something that once crossed over might not be crossed back again. It reminded him of the cobweb fence and the door into the Roach Motel through which Floyd had never returned. Clarence shuddered. Wouldn't he, if he went beyond the line, also be doing something forbidden? And might that bring him to a similar end?

But as he considered this, another thought grew in Clarence's mind. In crossing the line, in leaving the shelf, he'd be moving from a small place of quarantine into a larger space, the kitchen, and then into the great unknown! Surely he'd miss what he'd leave behind—his home, his family—and surely there were risks. Yet pausing there, he could feel his heart pushing him forward.

As quietly as he could, he went and kissed the bell of the candlesnuffer. In her sleep, his mother whimpered. To her, though she may not have heard, he whispered, "I'll be back soon. I promise."

Briefly he prayed for strength and fortitude. Then, clenching the shard of glass in his teeth and the string in his hands, he stepped across the line and over the edge.

15 / A Perilous Journey

It was not an easy descent. Clarence squeezed the string with his bare shins. His palms chafed and burned. And all the while, as he let himself down hand over hand, he kept swinging, twisting, and bumping—first against the edge of the lower shelf, then against a knob on the stove, and finally against the chrome handle of the oven. But he made it, leaping off the string just before he'd touched the floor. With the shard of glass, he cut the string. Then he took the string's bottom end, and, with a snapping motion that traveled upward in the shape of an S, unhooked the top end from the neck of the teapot. He stood clear as the string came hurtling down. He gathered it up and wound it neatly around his left shoulder, so that he made a bold and manly figure—except, of course, for his boxer shorts.

As he strode toward the oak threshold of the open doorway that led into the living room, he had a disturbing thought. *What if I fail? What if I don't come back? Who will alert everyone to the danger of the exterminator?*

He veered toward the dishwasher. Inside the crack where it met the floor, Willie lived with his parents and his kid sister in a nice, cozy home of dust and crumbs. Clarence knocked softly on the bottom edge of the dishwasher, using the secret code that only he and Willie knew: *tap . . . ta-tap-tap . . . tap-tap.*

He waited. He knocked again. He heard someone moving inside. Soon two familiar, wispy antennae edged out of the crack and stopped.

"Who is it?" came Willie's voice. It was the faintest whisper.

"Me," Clarence whispered back.

Willie's antennae edged out a little farther, and then Clarence saw the rest of him. His face was sleepy and scared. "How can I tell it's really you?" Willie asked. "You don't look like yourself anymore."

"Who else knows our special code? Who else has been your friend forever?"

"Well, aren't you supposed to be on the top shelf?" Willie said. "My parents told me not to go near you. They said you're contagious."

"But I have to tell you something!" Clarence replied.

"Shhh. You'll wake them up. Shouldn't you go back to the shelf? We'll see each other when you get better."

"I can't!" Clarence said, exasperated. "Listen. You're the only one I can trust."

Willie glanced over his shoulder. "All right. But could you take a few steps back?"

Clarence backed up, and Willie, keeping his distance, took a few cautious steps away from the crack, so they might talk without waking anyone.

Now Clarence told Willie about the phone call he'd overheard, and that an exterminator would be there early the next morning.

Willie didn't say anything, but his face turned white, and his eyes bugged out like a bee's.

"So I'm going to get help," Clarence continued. "I'm going on a journey. If I'm not back by dawn, you'll have to tell everyone to leave the kitchen. If I can't get help and the exterminator comes, no one will survive here!"

Willie looked confused. "But where would we all go . . . unless we leave the building? There are snakes and cats out there. They'll get us."

"It's our only chance," Clarence said. "If it comes to that."

They were both silent for a moment.

Staring at Clarence's shard of glass and coil of string, Willie asked, "This journey you're going on—it won't be far? You won't be going beyond the threshold, will you?"

Clarence nodded yes.

"But it's against the rules!"

"But I *have* to go!" Clarence insisted. "And if I

don't return, you've *got* to tell everyone. And then, *you've* got to leave, too!" He glanced at the clock. "Will you do that? Please."

Just then they heard someone moving beneath the dishwasher. Willie's parents were waking up, as was everyone else in the kitchen.

Willie scooted back inside the crack. Clarence hurried to the doorway, where he climbed to the top of the threshold, a place he'd never been before. Quickly, he surveyed what lay before him. In the glow of a night-light plugged into a wall, he saw a vast, dense forest of carpeting, interrupted here and there by thick legs of furniture. To the right stood a massive TV and a sofa, and dead ahead, across the opening of the hallway to the bedrooms, the dark bulk of a mountain rose up. It was Sparky, sprawled and sleeping. How would Clarence get around *that*?

Over his shoulder, he took one last look at the kitchen, as the moon washed over the stove, the counters, the shelves—the only home he'd ever known. Then, wielding his shard of glass like a sword, he waded into the carpeting. Gnarled and thorny, it reached to his chest. It raked his shins and stomach.

But step by step, he hacked, pushed, and chopped it down, making a narrow path. He went around a wicker wastebasket and avoided a sneaker on its side, a cavern of foul odor. Between the legs of a coffee table and the sofa, he came upon bits of Fritos and potato chips, hanging like trash in the foliage. He crossed the Sports page, which lay partially under the sofa. He came to a swampy place, smelling of stale beer, where the muck oozed between his toes, then sucked him down, thigh deep. *What slobs humans can be!*

Dirty and exhausted, he crawled onto solid land
again. There the carpet was matted with dog hair, and
funny, wingless, humpbacked bugs leaped around
him, as if on pogo sticks. Clarence guessed they were
something called "fleas." With Sparky as their plenti-
ful source of food, they were an energetic bunch, their
long back legs as springy as any grasshopper's.

In his squeaky voice, Clarence called out to them as
they bounced around, his head bobbing to keep them

in view. "Excuse me. Excuse me. Could you tell me how to get by this dog?"

"Usually we just hop right over," one of them said, smiling, as he winked at his friends, "but you don't look like much of a leaper." Still bouncing, they laughed, which made Clarence feel embarrassed and discouraged, and made him look down at his spindly legs. Would he have to turn back? Would all his efforts be for nothing?

Then another flea, who must have felt sorry for Clarence, piped up. He said that Clarence could sneak around Sparky's shoulder when Sparky raised his head to chew at a fleabite. "As it happens, I'm about to grab a bite from his front leg," the flea said. "So get ready to go."

Clarence thanked him, and sure enough, a moment later Sparky's head jerked up, and a narrow way opened, like a mountain pass, between the baseboard and the dog's hulking shoulder. Before it closed again, Clarence ran through it.

On the other side, he looked about, and he seemed to be in a different land, a desert. It was flat, dry, and treeless. Another carpet, the color of oatmeal, was worn in a wide, hard path down the middle of the hall. Here the going was easier, and now he thought he was making good progress, though distances were hard to measure, and he felt exposed and vulnerable, with no place to hide. To his left, he passed a dark study and then a bathroom with a scent of lilac shampoo. To the right, he saw a glow from another room, which he approached on tiptoe. Craning his neck around the edge of the doorway, he looked inside. He saw Larry in his striped pajamas sleeping like someone swimming the sidestroke. Beside him, Kathryn was reading a book. A page snapped as she turned it, and when her eyes shifted to the right-hand page, Clarence saw his chance. As fast as he could, he darted across the doorway—he made it!—and continued on his mission.

Now Mimi's room was the only one left. Her closed door, a towering rectangle, filled up the dark end of the hall, with a slice of light along its lower edge. He approached it as you might approach a cathedral, with a quiet, trembling awe. This was his destination, where he meant to go, and where he must find help.

But how would he get in? The brass doorknob was too high for him to lasso, and he wouldn't be able to turn the knob anyway. Should he boldly knock or call Mimi's name? But if he yelled loudly enough for her to hear him, wouldn't Kathryn hear him, too? What trouble that would bring!

Recalling some of his flattening techniques as a roach, he decided to squeeze under the door. First he pushed the coil of string and the shard of glass in front of him. Then he lay on his stomach, splaying his arms and legs, and blew all the breath from his body. He squirmed forward, grunting and scratching. He got his head under the door, as well as his chest and waist. But that was as far as he could go. He'd forgotten about his bottom, that silly double bump on his backside that was always following him around. No matter how hard he struggled, it wouldn't squash down and come through! Instead, his struggling just wedged it in tighter, until, with his feet in the hall and his head almost in Mimi's room, he could hardly move at all. What would happen if someone opened the door just then? Would he be dragged across the floor? Or squashed like a fly beneath a swatter?

Desperately, he clawed with his hands and kicked his legs.

But he was stuck.

16 / A Conversation

Yikes!"

It was Mimi's voice. She must have heard the grunting, scratching sounds of Clarence's exertions. From his cramped and embarrassing position, he saw the side of her cheek pressed to the wood floor an inch away on the other side of the door. Her big eye, round as a button, was peering at him. "Who—or what—are you?!"

"I'm Clarence Cochran. A boy."

She seemed astonished. "A boy?"

"Yes."

"But how can that be? You're so . . . small! I've never seen a boy so small, not even Timmy Garland in my science class. Don't boys have to be a certain size to be boys?"

Clarence didn't know what to say.

Mimi went on, "I've heard of stunted growth, but this is incredible! What could have caused it? Something genetic? Something in the environment?"

Mimi kept asking questions and using words that Clarence couldn't understand, so finally he blurted out, "Could I speak with you? Would you mind if I came in?"

Gamely, he tried once more to wriggle through on his own, but he was still stuck. He couldn't do it.

"Just a minute," Mimi said. He couldn't see her eye anymore. She must have gotten up and pulled upward on the knob, raising the door a fraction, because suddenly his bottom came free and he was able to slide his whole self into her room.

Clarence stood, picked up his shard of glass and coil of string, and dusted himself off as best he could. He took a step back and twisted his neck so he could see the full height of her. *Whoa!* She seemed so much taller than she did when he looked down on her from the kitchen shelf. Her legs disappeared into that very

long T-shirt, and her head was way, way up there. She'd undone her ponytail to take her shower, so her hair fell down the sides of her face in long, damp waves. Evidently Clarence had interrupted her as she was writing, for she held a pen in one hand, and on the nightstand, near an alarm clock, lay an open journal, facedown. Of course he'd often seen curious scribbles on the pad on the kitchen table, marks he now realized were words, like "milk," "eggs," or "hot dogs." But to write in a leather-bound journal! And with a pen! Whatever she wrote must be *very* important.

"I'm sorry to trouble you," he said to Mimi, remembering to be courteous. He stood up as tall as he could. His eyes were just above the level of her toenails, which he noticed were clean and neatly trimmed. This made him painfully aware of the smudges on his boxer shorts and the dried muck on his legs. "I'm also sorry that I'm such a mess," he went on. "I don't usually look like this, but I've been on a long journey, all the way from the kitchen, with some obstacles here and there."

Mimi peered at him intently. To say the least, she

was curious about him. Moreover, as she studied his small yet proud and plucky figure, her eyes appeared to soften, and her heart may have as well. She kneeled down so she could better address him. "Well, for someone who's traveled all that way, you don't look so unpresentable. By the way, my name is Miriam, though I'd rather you call me Mimi."

"Pleased to meet you, Mimi," he said, putting out his hand.

"My pleasure, as well," she said, as she reached down and ever so carefully extended her pinky toward him. With both his hands, he gripped her finger, practically hanging from it, and in this way they shook.

"I should get straight to my point," he said, worried that time was running out. "I'm wondering if you might help me with something."

"Why don't we sit down," she replied. She gestured toward the edge of her bed, which looked like the most comfortable and visible place for a small person to sit in her room. "Can I help you up?"

He said, "No, thank you," and while she settled herself cross-legged on the floor beside the bed, he scrambled over books and clothes, lassoed the bedpost, and pulled himself up like a mountaineer. He walked briskly along her bedspread and sat with his legs over the edge, where he and Mimi could see each other eye to eye.

"So what would you like to talk about?" she asked.

"Survival," he said simply.

This made her tilt her head and lean forward. "Survival? Whose survival?"

"Mine. And my family's. And the survival of my people, though they're not exactly people."

"What do you mean?"

With his voice inching higher, he told her how he'd once been a cockroach, until one evening he found himself turned into the boy who was now sitting before her. He told her about the light that went on in the middle of the night, and Mimi said, "I remember that." Then, to make a long story short, he told her how yesterday morning he'd heard her mother talking on the phone with an exterminator who'd be there the next morning. "Your parents," he said, looking right at Mimi, "are planning to kill us all!"

This made Mimi sit bolt upright. "Are you sure?"

"I'm positive."

Now she looked horrified. "This is terrible! Those exterminators should be put out of business! Spraying those pesticides. And to think, my own parents . . ." She paused, her eyes blazing like cobalt. "They can't do it! I won't let them! No exterminator can come here!"

Clarence was swept up in her determination. Besides the question of his own survival, this was about "our care for the earth" and "the living together of all beings," as Mimi so beautifully put it. Her parents would understand that. They had to! Mimi would see to it right away.

"I don't know how to thank you," he said.

She stood up. Then she did something he didn't expect. Gently, she scooped him off the edge of the bed, and for a second it was like that dizzy-happy *wheee-eee* feeling when he swung on the lamp's beaded pull-string with Willie. Then she just held him still in the cup of her hand, like a tiny bird in a nest. Her palm was pleasantly warm without being sticky. He felt comfortable and protected there, almost the way he used to feel when he lay deep in his crevice. She held him very close to her face, so that even her freckles seemed big, and he could smell the peppermint toothpaste on her breath and see her fine, almost clear lashes, and the black rays in the blue of her eyes, like spokes in a bright wheel.

"Try not to worry. It'll be all right," she said. "I'll take care of it." She set him on the nightstand, between the journal and the alarm clock. "Wait here." Then, with her back straight and head high, she walked out of her room, shutting the door behind her.

17 / A Disappointment

Soon Clarence heard the sounds of a serious discussion coming from Mimi's parents' bedroom. "Exterminators spray poisonous chemicals that don't disappear," Mimi said in her reasonable but forceful voice. "Those chemicals keep building up in the environment. They pollute the air, rivers, and streams."

Though Clarence couldn't make out the exact words, he heard her mother's measured tone, and then Mimi's voice louder than before: "That's against everything I believe in—and what I thought you believed in, too."

"Yes, but we have to do *something*," Kathryn replied. "Something that really works."

They went back and forth like this, the temperature heating up on both sides, with Mimi's father, jolted from sleep, complaining, "It's after midnight! What could be worth arguing about at this hour?"

But Mimi stood firm. "You shouldn't do it."

And her mother, equally firm, said, "There's no other way."

Meanwhile, Clarence paced back and forth on the nightstand in Mimi's bedroom. He had thought humans were better than this at solving their differences.

". . . Why? Because cockroaches spread disease," Mimi's mother said, her words now as loud as Mimi's. "Do you remember how sick you were the other day? It was probably because of them."

This must have struck a nerve in Mimi. "You can't prove that!"

"Well, just think. They're filthy. They live in sewers. They eat almost anything and track around whatever they step in. Why do you think everyone hates them?"

"They're living things!" Mimi cried. "They're just doing what they have to do to provide for themselves and their families! What would *you* do if you were one of them? *You* should think about *that*!"

This, Clarence thought, would surely hit home, but he was disappointed.

"We're talking about cockroaches, not people," Kathryn said flatly.

"Well, how are you so sure they're all filthy?" Mimi asked. "You don't really know them. In fact, they're usually neat and clean. Some of them you might even *like*! Have you ever met a cockroach?"

"Of course not!" Her mother's patience was gone. "Mimi, this is ridiculous! It's late, we're all tired, and I have to get up early!"

"You're not even listening to me!" Mimi shouted. "You won't hear what you don't agree with. It's like I don't even *exist*!"

"Go to bed, young lady," her mother said firmly. "End of conversation!"

Everything was quiet for a moment. Then Clarence heard the door of Mimi's parents' room slam. In an instant, the air *whooshed* as Mimi's door flew open, and she stomped in, her eyes red and streaming. She slammed the door behind her and, in two lunging steps, threw herself across the bed, burying her face in the pillow, her whole body heaving with sobs.

"They just don't understand!" she cried. "They won't listen!" Then, over and over: "I'm sorry. I'm sorry. I'm sorry."

When she paused, panting and exhausted, he managed to say to her, "You did your best. That's all you can do." His voice was quiet, without expression. Suddenly, he didn't feel bold anymore.

"I tried," she moaned. "I tried and tried and tried . . ."

"I know," he said gratefully. Sitting now on the cover of her journal with his elbows on his knees, he held his head in his hands. "But maybe there are things you can't change no matter how hard you try."

Mimi moaned again. She lifted her head from the pillow and turned to him. "You're talking about your own death!" Her nose was running. Her hair was a mess, stringy and matted with tears. Each of her eyes was a long, dark tunnel with only a speck of light far away.

"Wait. I know!" she said, still weeping but brightening a little. "You can stay here with me! I'll never let anything happen to you, Clarence. I promise. My room can be your home!"

This touched Clarence and almost made him cry, too. He told Mimi how much he appreciated her words. He told her what a good, generous person she was, and how, if he'd never been a roach and had never lived with his family, he might take her up on her offer. "But I can't stay here," he said. "My family would miss me, and I'd miss them."

He gathered up his shard of glass and coil of string, then stood to leave.

"We could bring your whole family here to live," Mimi said, sitting up on the bed.

"What would your parents say about that?" he asked. "And for me, there's everyone else in the kitchen to think about—even though many of them don't like me, now that I'm changed."

"But you don't even look like them," Mimi pleaded. "You look more like me, and you act like me, and you think like me! Do you know what I'm going to write in my journal next time? I'm going to write that I've met the most extraordinary person, who's so polite and sensitive, who doesn't make fun of my ideas, a person who could be my true friend and maybe sort of like a brother—and I could be a sister to him. Clarence, you're not a cockroach anymore. You're a boy!"

He thought of sitting in the warm cup of her hand. Then he thought of his mother's touch and the slow, willowy sway of her antennae, and the way she'd look at him when she first saw him every evening, as if she hadn't seen him in a long time. On this point, Mimi wasn't altogether right. Yes, he *was* a boy, a human boy, but in some deep part of him, he would always be a cockroach.

"You have to remember," he said in his own pleading voice, "I didn't begin my life like this. I didn't look like this. I didn't grow up like this. My parents don't look like this. And my brothers . . ."

For a while he couldn't say anything, and he couldn't meet her eyes, even though he could tell by the way she nodded that she understood what he was feeling. In a thin voice, he eventually said, "I need to go home."

"I'll take you," she said bravely, her lower lip trembling.

But he didn't think she should go down to the kitchen in the middle of the night when the roaches would be out on the counters—they'd had enough surprises. And besides, he was a proud little person. He would take care of himself. He'd asked enough of her already. "No," he said, shaking his head sadly. "Thanks. But no."

He secured his string around the alarm clock and, hand over hand, let himself down to the floor as she watched. "Farewell," he said, polite to the end.

And with that, he waved goodbye.

18 / A Big Idea

With so much dreary news in his heart, Clarence's return trip to the kitchen took a very long time. He trudged past the dark rooms along the hall and across the barren desert. With his friend the flea's help, he edged around Sparky again. He slogged through the swamp, pushed and hacked through the living room carpet, and finally climbed, almost crawling, over the threshold. He knew that even with his clever tools and ingenuity, he couldn't make it up to the shelves he called "home"—he'd never scale the enameled front of the stove—so he left his shard of glass and coil of string beneath the radiator. With what seemed like his last ounce of strength, he shinnied up the lamp's electric cord and got onto the table where he'd have a view of the whole kitchen.

What he saw made him both grateful and dismayed. Willie *had* alerted everyone, after all. The dawn was glimmering through the window. Birds were chirping. It was seven a.m., and the roaches were all scurrying this way and that, getting ready to leave!

The shelves, corners, and backs of counters teemed with neighbors, friends, and acquaintances, collecting their possessions and loved ones. Using a curl of pencil-shaving as a megaphone, the mayor was shouting out instructions: they were all to leave through the window, go down the side of the building, and reassemble in the courtyard.

So busy and frenzied was everyone that no one even noticed Clarence. On their backs they were piling bits of cloth, morsels of food, scraps of paper, pins, toothpicks, matches—anything they could get their claws on. Some carried purse-shaped egg cases ready to hatch, and nymphs who wailed and wailed. The old and infirm staggered with their canes. *Will they be left behind?* Clarence wondered. *Who will take care of them?* And everywhere was a smell, something sharp and coppery, that Clarence knew meant fear.

Then, from shelves and shadowy backs of counters . . . from under the dishwasher and the stove . . . from behind the backsplash . . . from around the doors of cabinets and drawers . . . from behind the pictures on the refrigerator . . . from inside the portable radio and the clock . . . from under the coffeemaker and the food processor . . . from cracks between strips of vinyl flooring . . . even from holes of electrical outlets— from *everywhere!*—more and more roaches came. They gathered into wider and wider streams . . . that fed into a wider and wider river . . . that flooded across walls and counters toward the kitchen window. A river of roach refugees!

Clarence saw Dr. Blatt stumbling and wheezing in the torrent, with his black bag clutched in his front claws. He saw the psychologist and physical therapist sprinting ahead, huffing through their airholes. He saw Reverend O'Coccus bringing up the rear, like a shepherd behind his frightened flock. In the midst of it all stood Police Chief Handleman, trying to maintain order while the crowd swelled and surged. Everyone was growing more desperate, forgetting their manners, and bumping and shoving.

Clarence saw his father across the kitchen on the

lower shelf above the stove. He was frantically collecting cracker crumbs and nuggets of cheese for the journey. Then Clarence saw two others he recognized, one on the lower shelf and one on the top. *Could it be true?* Stephen had returned home from wherever he'd been! And his mother was out from under the candlesnuffer!

Stephen's back was piled with his important things, and his mother's face was distraught. She kept looking back toward the crevice and then at the crowd, her eyes searching and searching.

"Mom!" Clarence screamed at the top of his lungs. His voice sailed over the din.

His mother spotted him. "Clarence! It's you! You're back! Wait for us! We're coming!"

Meanwhile, hearing Clarence's scream, everyone else in the kitchen stopped. From Willie, they must have learned of Clarence's journey, for they turned and looked at Clarence, their antennae stiff and attentive, their eyes full of hope and fear. Had he stopped the exterminator from coming? Had he saved them?

Those hundreds of eyes froze Clarence in place, with his arms hanging at his sides. All he could do was open his hands and turn his palms out, as if to show they were empty.

Disgusted, the crowd turned away, and the wild shoving toward the window continued. Then Clarence saw Willie near the front of the crowd. He was waving to Clarence, at once beckoning and desperately trying to make his way toward him. He called, "Clarence, I did it—I told them to leave! Hurry! We need to get out!"

And Clarence, waving back, yelled, "Thanks, Willie. I'm waiting to go with my family."

But Willie, it seemed, couldn't hear, as the tide swept him farther away.

Now Clarence's mother, who had scampered down the wall and squeezed through the rear of the crowd, arrived on the tabletop. Apparently the quarantine was over—it didn't matter anymore. She rushed to him and they embraced, her legs and antennae wrapping around him like spaghetti around a fork. "I was thinking so much about Floyd," she said, "that I almost lost sight of what we still have, even if we might only have it for a little while longer." She unwrapped her antennae from around Clarence, stepped back, and looked him in the eye. "But now I see it again."

In a moment, Clarence's father and Stephen arrived, sweating, panting, and top-heavy with their loads. Their faces were white as milk.

Clarence's father gave him a quick hug, then said to

his family, "Look at the sky! It's getting brighter! Soon we'll be blind as bats!"

"And soon we'll be drowning in poison!" Stephen said. "I'm getting out of here!"

"If we leave, we're leaving with one another," their mother said. "What matters is that we're together."

Clarence looked around at the kitchen and then at each member of his family: his father with his strong but shaking legs; his brother revving his wings as if he could fly away; and his mother in the gray light, standing still and thoughtful, as if figuring out what was best for the family.

Clarence's heart quaked with love and sorrow. *Here are the ones I know best on this earth, and I have failed them.* His journey had been fruitless. He'd been wrong about Mimi—she *couldn't* help. But something inside him wouldn't give up. *Something just has to be done!*

Still looking at his family, he felt a shiver in all his bones, right down to the tips of his fingers. His skin tingled. His hands itched. And suddenly he had a big idea, the biggest of his whole life! In an instant, it seemed to bloom inside him and fill up his head.

There on the table lay the pad of paper. On top was the stubby pencil. As his family watched, Clarence walked to the pencil, bent down, and, with a grunt, picked up the eraser end.

"Let's get going!" his brother pleaded.

"Come on!" his father cried.

"No. Wait," his mother replied, nodding at Clarence. "I think he has something in mind."

Spreading his legs for balance, Clarence leaned the

pencil against his shoulder, with the point still on the paper. Held there with his arms hooped around it, the pencil seemed poised, as did he. It felt alive, full, weighty, and waiting. It almost felt like part of *him*. Holding it felt awkward, but right.

Now he began to think of everything that had been happening recently and everything that he'd been feeling. And as he felt these things, they made him move, and as he moved, he did something no roach had ever done or thought of:

He wrote.

19 / The Letter

And what he wrote was this:

Dear Mrs. Gilmartin,

Standing on the pad, Clarence glanced back in amazement at what he'd written. Somehow the letters and words had come out of him, and together they even made sense! He lifted the pencil and, hefting it over his shoulder, walked back to the left-hand side of the pad where he put down the point again. Then, as he moved to the right, stumbling with the heavy pencil, whole strings of words—sentences!—followed him:

My name is Clarence Cochran, and I want to tell you about my life. I was born and grew up as a cockroach. Then I changed into a little boy. But I still love my cockroach family.

With the word *"family,"* a whole flood of feelings rushed into him, funneled down into the pencil point, and spilled onto the pad. Now he couldn't stop moving, even if he wanted to. Back and forth he went! The words and sentences just kept coming, and they seemed to pour straight from his heart. He was writ-ing! He was speaking up for himself! And he had a lot to say:

Once my family and I lived together in a nice home in this nice kitchen, but now everything is different. A few days ago, I had a brother named Floyd, but he isn't here anymore. He disappeared in the Roach Motel, which I saw you take out to the trash. That made my father angry, and it made my brother Stephen run away. It made me scared, and most of all it made my mother very sad. She kept calling Floyd's name—over and over. Can you imagine that?

Clarence had to pause. This rush of writing was ex-hausting and brought tears to his eyes, a number of which fell on the pad, leaving tiny stains, especially where he wrote "Floyd" and "mother." But he pulled himself together. Watching him, his family stood speechless. He wiped his eyes with the heel of one hand, lifted the pencil, and continued:

Soon the exterminator that you called will be here, and if he does what he's supposed to do, we'll all be dead. I hope that dying won't hurt too much. I hope it won't take too long. Maybe after it's over, we'll be with Floyd again. That's what Reverend O'Coccus tells us, but I'm not so sure. How will I recognize Floyd in heaven if he doesn't have his body with him, if he's just a soul, like the Reverend says? How will I recognize Stephen? Or my father? Or how will I even know my mother, if I can't feel her antennae around me, or hear her voice, or see her face, or smell her special smell? How will she know me?

Clarence had come to the bottom of the page. He stepped off the pad and set down the pencil. He read what he'd written aloud to his family. With the help of his brother, he tore the page off the pad. His mother, in particular, seemed deeply moved by his words. She dabbed at her eyes with a bit of Kleenex. "Ralph, I've never heard of such a thing, but

I think we have a writer in the family! Isn't that strange?"

Now climbing onto the pad with his pencil again, Clarence swallowed down the lump in his throat and finished his letter:

When I die, I will miss a lot of things. Like sweet-and-sour pork. Like kicking the pea back and forth with Willie. I'll miss Mimi, too, with her big ideas and her crazy hair. And I'll miss the way the moon moves across the sky when I watch it from the windowsill.

I wish that we didn't have to die. I wish, Mrs. Gilmartin, that we could find a way for us all to live together.

Sincerely,
Clarence Cochran

P.S. Tell Mimi good luck. She is a wonderful person.

20 / A Knock on the Door

Together the Cochran family tore the second page off the pad and stood for a moment admiring Clarence's letter.

"It's a good letter," Clarence's father said. "Very convincing. But considering who it's written to, how can it change anything?" He shielded his eyes and looked anxiously around the kitchen again. "We've got to get out of here. Almost everyone else has gone!"

Meanwhile, Clarence was shaking with the strain of writing his letter. He'd put everything he had into it, and now all he could do was wonder: *Will Kathryn Gilmartin even read it? Will she read it before the ex-*

terminator comes? And if she does, what will happen?

Though the sun hadn't quite edged over the building across the courtyard, it was definitely morning. Things in the kitchen were taking on color. Clarence could smell coffee brewing and bacon frying in the apartment below, and from somewhere beyond the courtyard came the faint rustle of traffic.

"It's time to go," his mother said sadly.

And Clarence knew she was right. There was nothing else he could do.

Leaving the letter on the table, they all hurried toward the lamp, where they would slide down the electric cord to the floor and from there make their way toward the window.

But they didn't get very far. They were crawling around the oval base of the sugar bowl, when Clarence's parents and brother suddenly stopped.

"Don't move!" his mother whispered.

In the next instant, Kathryn Gilmartin stepped into the room.

From where Clarence stood behind the sugar bowl, peeking one eye around its side, he could see her clearly. Since it was Saturday, she was wearing her gray sweatshirt and pants. As she came through the doorway, she didn't turn on the overhead light. She went to the fridge and, pouring a glass of orange juice, glanced at the clock.

It was seven-fifty. Ten minutes until the exterminator would be there.

She brought the juice to the table and sat with one arm so near to the sugar bowl that Clarence could almost reach out and touch her. She drank most of the juice. She yawned with her hand over her mouth. Finally she noticed the letter.

She picked it up. Clarence's handwriting was so small and clumsy that she had to look hard to understand what she was holding. Reaching across the table, she pulled the beaded string of the lamp, which made Clarence and his family squinch even closer to the back of the sugar bowl.

Up this close, Clarence could see that Kathryn was very tired, as if she hadn't slept after her argument with Mimi. Her face looked as worn and gray as her sweatshirt, but when she pushed her hair behind her ears, there was still that scary, determined angle of her jaw. She began to read the letter.

As she did, her eyebrows knit together with interest. *This could be a good sign,* Clarence thought. But
then a small smile passed across Kathryn's lips, as
though she didn't believe what she was reading and
had recognized a clever trick. Perhaps she thought
Mimi had written the letter, imitating a younger kid's
awkward handwriting and trying in another way to
change her mother's mind. For a time, the letter
seemed to amuse Kathryn, and it annoyed Clarence
that someone would make light of his heartfelt words.
It was all he could do to keep from crying out, *Those
are my words! Every one!*

Then, as she finished the first page and moved on to the second, a stillness slowly came over her face. She didn't look as certain as she'd been. There was no sign of amusement anymore. Her mouth was a short, straight line. Her eyes stayed glued to the pad. With her chin in one palm, she took a long time to finish.

When she was done, she looked up, and, moving only her eyes, peered around, listening intently, as if she thought someone might be watching her. Clarence didn't breathe. His heart didn't seem to beat. At last, she put the letter aside, spread her fingers on the table, and stared at the tops of her hands.

Then, there was a knock on the door.

21 / A Reply

Startled from her thoughts, Kathryn pushed her chair away from the table, got up, and walked into the living room. She turned toward the apartment door, disappearing from Clarence's sight.

"Quick, let's run for it!" Stephen whispered.

But Clarence's parents shook their heads. What was the use? It was broad daylight, and they could barely see. They wrapped their antennae around each other and both their remaining sons.

Clarence heard the *click* as Kathryn turned the dead bolt on the front door. He heard the *clink, clink* as she unhitched the safety chain. Next came the deeper *clunk* as she turned the doorknob. He heard the door squeak on its hinges. Then Kathryn must have stepped into the hall, for Clarence could only hear the courteous tone of her voice—he couldn't hear her words themselves—as she spoke with someone.

It was just a short conversation, and the voice of the other person, a man, sounded mild, Clarence thought, for an exterminator. It also sounded confused. At one point, Clarence *did* hear him say, "I thought you wanted . . ." And later the man said, "Yes, ma'am, whatever you say."

Then there was a moment of silence.

Then the hinges squeaked, the door closed, the dead bolt clicked, and the safety chain clinked into place.

Then Kathryn returned to the kitchen. Alone!

Clarence blinked and shook his head. *Can I believe my eyes?*

Even then, he couldn't tell what Kathryn was thinking, though something must have been on her mind, for she'd forgotten to bring in the newspaper. She sat down and finished her juice. Again she glanced around, listening carefully. By now the sun had climbed over the building beyond the courtyard, its light flooding across the table—on the lamp, on the sugar bowl where Clarence and his family hid in the shadows, and on the pad of paper which Kathryn now slid directly in front of her.

Clarence watched her pick up the stubby pencil. Small though it was, it fit neatly between her fingers and thumb. She put the point on the pad. For an instant, it seemed impossibly balanced, like a gyroscope on a string. Then it skated in long strides across the paper, so beautifully and effortlessly, the letters tilting, curving, looping, gliding, and flowing one into another. Clarence stood on tiptoes to see. This is what he read:

Dear Clarence Cochran,
    Thank you for your letter, which I've read with surprise and curiosity. For a cockroach, you are quite a good writer.

You have expressed your interest in finding a way for us all to live together. I don't know if that can happen, especially between such different groups. As I'm sure you know, humans and cockroaches have a long history. We've never gotten along.

Still, I have been a wife, a mother, and a teacher for too many years to rule out even the most unlikely of possibilities.

So let's try.

I look forward to hearing from you.

Sincerely,
Kathryn Gilmartin

Here the pencil point paused above the pad, and Clarence thought that Kathryn had finished the letter. But then she added a few more words:

P.S. Please tell your mother I'm very sorry about your brother Floyd.

22 / An Agreement

O ver the next five or six nights, the cockroaches were quietly relieved and nervously hopeful. All of them, including Willie, had returned safely to the kitchen when they'd heard that the exterminator had been sent away. In church, Reverend O'Coccus offered prayers of thanksgiving. Everyone was on their best behavior. And during this period, Clarence and Kathryn Gilmartin wrote letters to each other in which they tried to come to an agreement. Clarence, advised by the mayor, wrote on the pad in the wee hours of the night, and Kathryn, with Mimi's input, wrote letters during the day. It was a long and difficult process, as both sides were still suspicious of one another. In their letters, Clarence and Kathryn exchanged many ideas, proposals, and counterproposals. Finally, by the next weekend, they'd reached a compromise that the Gilmartin family and the cockroach Town Council approved in separate day and night ceremonies.

For all to see, the agreement itself, in Clarence's handwriting, was stuck with smiley-face magnets to the front of the refrigerator. In keeping with its serious tone, it was called "*A Solemn Statement of Agreement.*"

In it, the cockroaches promised to never go in the silverware drawer, on the table, on plates, in cups, glasses, or in "*any other eating, drinking, or cooking container for humans that we can't think of right now.*"

For their part, the Gilmartins agreed to share the sink with the cockroaches and to put out a small paper dish of spoiled food each evening, plus a half teaspoon of *fresh* food, a point that Clarence insisted on and that very much puzzled Kathryn. The Gilmartins also agreed to leave the cockroaches' shelves and drawers undisturbed, and under no circumstances would they set out bait traps, spray poison, *"or pay anyone else to do bad things to the cockroach community."*

Finally, the Gilmartins agreed to buy, and the cockroaches agreed to take care of, *"one small potted houseplant that will forever stay on the kitchen windowsill and be called the Floyd Cochran Memorial Garden."*

Below those words, all the Gilmartins had written their names, and the members of the Town Council, after dipping their feet in ink, had solemnly left their claw marks. Then, at the very end, Clarence had written *"Faithfully recorded"* and proudly signed his own name, which was followed by a crisp comma and an old-fashioned word that seemed to suit him: *"Scribe."*

23 / The End

If this were a fairy tale and not an honest-to-God true story, you might expect that, after Clarence and Kathryn had achieved their historic agreement and nothing heroic remained for him to do, Clarence would turn back into a cockroach and comfortably return to his former life. Perhaps one evening he'd wake up to see two long poles—his antennae!—swaying like fishing rods before him. He might feel his shell surrounding him like a pod. Along his sides, he'd breathe through his airholes, which would give off that musty, cheesy aroma that meant *I belong*. Then he'd look down and see his six legs, the same as every other cockroach. There they'd be! Every one! Each leg barbed, wiry, triple-jointed, claw-footed, and dabbed with that special gummy goo that could give him traction anywhere!

But things don't always turn out the way they do in fairy tales. You can't always return to who you were, at least not in real life. Those visions of turning back into a roach were just that—visions, Clarence's vivid dreams—and when he awoke from them, he saw his thin chest, his pale arms attached to his shoulders, and his two spindly legs sticking out of his plaid boxer shorts. *I am still a boy in the crevice,* he realized, *a human boy among cockroaches.*

Which meant that the future would bring difficulties and challenges for Clarence. He would never run on walls and ceilings again, and he would never impress the females his age with his six-clawed fancy footwork or by pumping up his wings. So how would he get a girlfriend? Would he ever be married? What sort of job could he get?

But Clarence tried not to think too much about all that. For now, he tried to live day to day. That was enough to think about, and on the whole things seemed to be going pretty well. While suspicions lingered, both sides were observing the compromise, which was a source of great pride for Clarence. His mother didn't hide anymore beneath the candle-snuffer, but spent her time knitting, housekeeping, tending the potted plant on the windowsill, and watching over the family. Using rope ladders that he and his father made from thread and matchstick rungs, Clarence was able to climb into and out of his crevice, and move from shelf to counter to cupboard, and participate in most family and community activities. Once again, Clarence kicked the pea for hours with Willie, who had apologized for not having been a true friend. Clarence had put his arms around Willie. Then they'd shaken earnestly, hand to claw, and once more were the best of pals.

During that time, Clarence also lived in another world. On evenings after the Gilmartins had finished cleaning up their dinner and had left a half teaspoon of fresh food on the counter, he would get up much earlier than the other roaches. He'd wash his face and comb his hair. Feeling shy and excited, he'd quietly climb out of his crevice and wait near the edge of the top shelf, with his cloth knapsack over his shoulder.

Since the compromise, Mimi had started doing her homework in the kitchen, a habit her parents thought odd—but then again, what *wasn't* odd about Mimi? When the TV went off in the living room and her parents had gone down the hall to their bedroom, Mimi would call good night to them and then whisper the words that Clarence listened for: "The coast is clear."

He'd climb down his rope ladder to join her. On the floor, the two of them would sprawl on their stomachs, head to head, with knees bent, feet in the air, and pencils and books strewn around. They'd read. Mimi would do her homework. They'd talk about all kinds of things: their friends, their parents, the shrinking of the polar ice caps. Then sometimes, before they'd say good night, Mimi would make her hand into a cup. Clarence would climb in, feeling warm and safe, and she'd hold him for a while.

And so the story of Clarence Cochran ends, though in fact it never *really* ends. Instead, it will always be told and retold from grandparent to parent to nymph. How and why Clarence turned from a roach into a human boy are today still topics of conversation along the windowsill, under the radiator, on the counter, and in the corner cabinet after church.

Of equal interest is what happened to Kathryn Gilmartin, her sudden willingness to make peace with the roaches she'd wanted dead. Mayor Grimes calls it a commonsense decision. In sermons, Reverend O'Coccus refers to it as an act of God. Others say it was blind luck, while Clarence's mother just calls it a great mystery, having to do with the depth of the heart—even human hearts—and the ability of us all to change.

J   Loizeaux, William.
FIC
Loizeaux   Clarence Cochran, a
           human boy.

DATE			